MISSION SURVIVAL

RAGE OF THE RHINO

www.randomhousechildrens.co.uk

CHARACTER PROFILES

Beck Granger

At just thirteen years old, Beck Granger knows more about the art of survival than most military experts learn in a lifetime. When he was young he travelled with his parents to some of the most remote places in the world, from Antarctica to the African Bush, and he picked up many vital survival skills from the remote tribes he met along the way.

Uncle Al

Professor Sir Alan Granger is one of the world's most respected anthropologists. His stint as a judge on a reality television show made him a household name in the UK, but to Beck he will always be plain old Uncle Al – more comfortable in his lab with a microscope than hob-nobbing with the rich and famous. He believes that patience is a virtue and has a 'never-say-die' attitude to life. For the past few years he has been acting as guardian to Beck, who has come to think of him as a second father.

David & Melanie Granger

Beck's mum and dad were Special Operations Directors for the environmental direct action group Green Force. Together with Beck, they spent time with remote tribes in some of the world's most extreme places. Several years ago their light plane crashed in the jungle, and wreckage was spread for miles around. To this day their bodies have never been found, and the cause of the accident remains unexplained . . .

Samora Peterson

Having grown up in South Africa with a father who works as a ranger in Kruger National Park, Samora was always destined to be pretty knowledgeable about wild animals. When she's not at school, she can usually be found with her dad studying migration patterns of elephants or helping to save rhinos and other endangered animals.

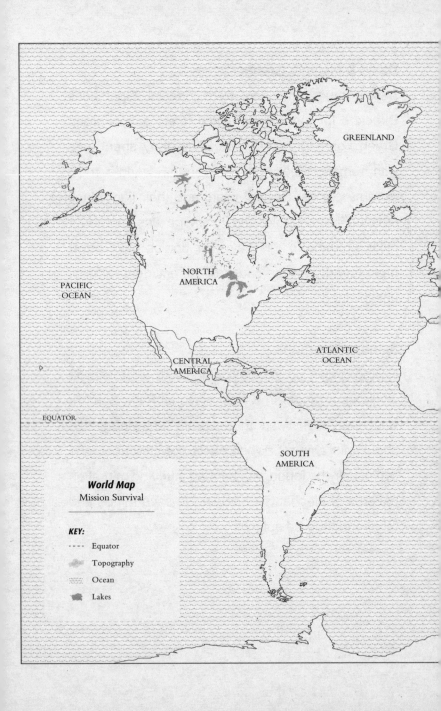

GREENLAND

NORTH
AMERICA

PACIFIC
OCEAN

ATLANTIC
OCEAN

CENTRAL
AMERICA

EQUATOR

SOUTH
AMERICA

World Map
Mission Survival

KEY:
- - - - Equator
Topography
Ocean
Lakes

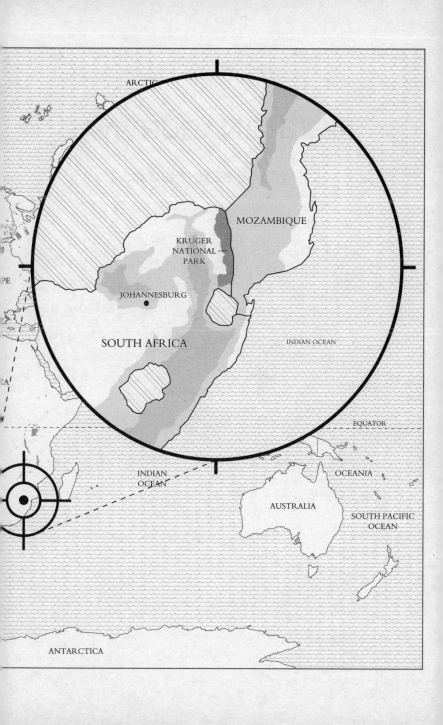

ARCTIC

MOZAMBIQUE

KRUGER
NATIONAL
PARK

JOHANNESBURG

SOUTH AFRICA

INDIAN OCEAN

PE

A

EQUATOR

INDIAN
OCEAN

OCEANIA

AUSTRALIA

SOUTH PACIFIC
OCEAN

ANTARCTICA

MISSION SURVIVAL

HAVE YOU READ THEM ALL?

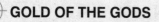

GOLD OF THE GODS

Location: The Colombian Jungle

Dangers: Snakes; sharks; howler monkeys

Beck travels to Colombia in search of the legendary City of Gold. Could a mysterious amulet provide the key to uncovering a secret that was thought to be lost for ever?

WAY OF THE WOLF

Location: The Alaskan Mountains

Dangers: Snow storms; wolves; white-water rapids

After their plane crashes in the Alaskan wilderness, Beck must stave off hunger and the cold as he treks through the frozen mountains in search of help.

SANDS OF THE SCORPION

Location: The Sahara Desert

Dangers: Diamond smugglers; heatstroke; scorpions

Beck is forced into the Sahara Desert to escape a gang of diamond smugglers. Can he survive the heat and evade the smugglers as he makes his way back to safety?

TRACKS OF THE TIGER

Location: The Indonesian Jungle

Dangers: Fiery lava flows; tigers; orang-utans

When a volcano eruption strands him in the jungles of Indonesia, Beck must pitch his survival skills against red-hot lava flows, a gang of illegal loggers, and the tigers that are on his trail . . .

CLAWS OF THE CROCODILE

Location: The Australian Outback

Dangers: Flash floods; salt-water crocodiles; Uranium leaks

Beck heads to the Outback in search of the truth about the plane crash that killed his parents. But somebody wants the secret to remain hidden – and they will kill to protect it.

STRIKE OF THE SHARK

Location: The Bermuda Triangle

Dangers: Tiger sharks; dehydration; hurricanes

When Beck is ship-wrecked in the open seas, he needs all of his survival skills to save a small group of passengers. But he soon discovers that the sinking was no accident . . .

RAGE OF THE RHINO
A RED FOX BOOK 978 1 782 95597 9

First published in Great Britain by Doubleday,
an imprint of Random House Children's Publishers UK
A Penguin Random House Company

Penguin
Random House
UK

Doubleday edition published 2014
Red Fox edition published 2015

Penguin Random House is committed to a sustainable future for our business,
our readers and our planet. This book is made from Forest Stewardship Council®
certified paper.

MIX
Paper from
responsible sources
FSC® C018179
www.fsc.org

Set in Swiss 721 BT

Red Fox Books are published by Random House Children's Publishers UK,
61–63 Uxbridge Road, London W5 5SA

www.**randomhousechildrens**.co.uk
www.**randomhouse**.co.uk

Addresses for companies within The Random House Group Limited can be found at:
www.randomhouse.co.uk/offices.htm

THE RANDOM HOUSE GROUP Limited Reg. No. 954009

A CIP catalogue record for this book is available from the British Library.

Printed and bound in Great Britain by CPI Group (UK) Ltd, Croydon, CR0 4YY

MISSION◉SURVIVAL
RAGE OF THE
RHINO

BEAR GRYLLS

RED FOX

To young Scouts all over the world.
Go for it in your lives and grab all those adventures.
And always live by the Scouting code, which will
help empower you to your full potential.
With admiration to you all,
Bear Grylls (Chief Scout)

Chapter 1

The first thing Beck Granger saw as he stepped into the kitchen was the caterpillar. And it was huge.

He stopped in his tracks, then bent down to inspect it more closely. It didn't move.

He had come in from school, chucked down his bags, made his way into the kitchen – and there it was. The caterpillar took up half the table. It was as long as Beck's forearm, its skin thick and green, and studded with spines.

At one end was a smiley face made of marzipan.

Beck looked up at his uncle. 'Ha ha.'

'I thought it would be right up your street, Beck!'

Uncle Al – Professor Sir Alan Granger, to anyone outside the family – applied a match to the caterpillar's spines, which were the candles.

Fourteen of them. 'It's in honour of all the insects you've managed to eat in fourteen years of life.'

'Mmm. Thanks for the reminder.'

Al extinguished the match with a flick of his wrist and put an arm around Beck's shoulders. Beck accepted the hug.

'Happy birthday! I have to say, there were times when I was afraid neither of us would be seeing this day.'

He said it lightly, but Beck heard the stress that lurked behind his words. Beck had never given much thought to birthdays – they just happened naturally, one after the other. But yes, there had been times during those fourteen years when he hadn't been sure he would live to see the next one.

Just recently, he had learned that there were people in the world determined to make sure he didn't even make it through to the next sunrise. So maybe he had more reason than most teenagers to celebrate.

He had a proper birthday party planned for the weekend, with friends his own age. Today it was just the two of them.

The candles were all lit.

'Make a wish?' Al suggested.

Beck thought for a moment, then bent down close to the cake and blew. The candles went out in one puff, and the wish was made.

Please make Al's friends get a move on!

The last three months had been an agony of routine and trying to be normal.

He had returned from an eventful cruise in the Caribbean. It had involved shipwrecks, exploding drilling rigs and murder. For the first time Beck had been able to put a name and a face to the organization that had killed his parents and blighted his life: Lumos.

He had known about Lumos for a long time. In his mind he had lumped it together with all the other corporations that were happy to see the Earth ruined, so long as they made money. But he hadn't realized just how bad Lumos was – rotten to the very core.

He had found that out when Lumos had put its most senior operative onto the job of killing him. She had failed; he and Al had returned to England . . . and done nothing.

At least, that was what it felt like. They *knew* about Lumos, but they couldn't *prove* anything. They needed hard evidence that would stand up in court. The only evidence they had was in their own heads.

Al had friends, and plenty of them, in the Green Force environmental action group. They believed the story. Al had been able to give them pointers to where to start looking for evidence of wrongdoing. But it all took time – so much time. And Green Force had other projects to be getting on with – like doing what it was meant to do, which was raise environmental awareness and fight ecological criminals all around the world.

Green force couldn't afford to throw everything it had at Lumos if it meant taking resources away from other jobs.

The result had been three long months of waiting, not knowing if Lumos would strike again.

For a while Al had checked under his car for bombs every day before heading off to work. Beck had been kept out of school on the pretext of being ill.

Eventually they had decided that Lumos wouldn't be quite so obvious. The company had their own reasons for lying low and not attracting attention – it wouldn't help their image if Beck suddenly turned up dead so soon after their previous encounter.

The last time they tried to kill Beck, they had lured him out of the country. As long as he and Al stayed at home, they should be safe.

So Beck went back to school again and tried to act like a normal schoolboy. But 'normal' was Beck's kind of living hell.

Chapter 2

'Looks like you got a lot of cards this year!'

Al's cheerful tone jolted Beck back to the present. His uncle passed him a sheaf of stiff envelopes. Beck leafed through them, looking at the postmarks and stamps to guess who they were from.

A stamp with a kangaroo and a Western Australia postmark – that was easy. That would be Brihony, though the kangaroo seemed out of place. Her speciality was saltwater crocodiles. Those had been just one of the dangers they'd encountered as they yomped across the Outback in search of the old man who could help them fight Lumos.

A stamp from Alaska, showing a pod of orcas diving below the surface of a smooth, cold sea, was from Tikaani, with whom he had hiked across frozen mountains to get help for a badly injured Al. That was the first time Beck had bumped into Lumos.

A kind of jungle scene from Colombia – that would be Christina and Marco, the twins who had survived a shipwreck and then a jungle trek with him on the trail of a drug lord.

And one with no stamp at all; just a hand-drawn picture of an orang-utan saying 'Hi, Beck!' That one had been hand delivered by Peter, his best friend, who only lived a few streets away.

Peter had not only been stranded with him in the Sahara, escaping from murderous diamond smugglers; he had also ended up dodging tigers and volcanoes in the Indonesian rainforest. After that, Peter's parents had been less enthusiastic about their son going on holiday with Beck. Even though Peter was always up for more.

Beck smiled. He had made a few enemies in fourteen years, but he made many more friends in the course of his adventures. Friends he would always treasure.

The smile dimmed a little. There was one boy he didn't expect to get a card from. He didn't even know if James Blake was still alive. When Beck last saw him, he had been sobbing as he tried to free his mother from the tangled wreckage on a collapsing drilling rig.

And why were they on the rig in the first place? Beck's smile dimmed further still. Lumos. Lumos, Lumos, Lumos – always Lumos, everywhere he looked. This time, they had been experimenting with a new fuel source on the sea bed. It could make them very rich, and at the same time it would cause devastation. Lumos only cared about the first bit. Beck had been there because James's mother was Lumos's assassin, acting under orders from James's grandfather, the head of Lumos, Edwin Blake. She had lured him onto the rig to kill him.

And why was the rig collapsing? Because, consumed with greed, Lumos had planted it right in the path of the biggest hurricane of the century. And, OK, Beck had helped the process by causing an underwater explosion, but that had been so he could escape. The explosion hadn't hurt anyone, and he wouldn't have needed to set it off if no one had been trying to kill him in the first place . . .

His mind whirled as he recalled the details.

Despite everything, Beck would have helped James to save his mother. He could have shown her that there was a better way than her sad, twisted, selfish view of life. But he had been prevented from doing this by someone bigger and stronger than him, who had dragged him away and thrown him into a helicopter. Soon after they'd taken off, the rig had exploded.

James might have survived, or he might be at the bottom of the sea.

Beck tried to put a stop to his wild thoughts and concentrated on his birthday cards.

There was one more which obviously came from abroad, but he couldn't place it. He couldn't even read the stamp. It wasn't the usual alphabet. There was something that was obviously an E, then two characters that looked like pyramids, then an A, then something like a wrong way round figure 3. He raised an eyebrow and showed it to Al.

'Hellas,' his uncle translated. 'Or, as you and I would call it, Greece.'

'Greece?' Beck frowned and stuck a finger under

the flap to open it. 'Who do I know in Greece?'

The envelope contained a card and a letter, hand-written in English. Beck read out the first line slowly, stumbling over the unfamiliar writing:

> 'Dear Beck,
> Happy birthday! You won't remember me, but we met when you were very little. My name is Athena Sapera—'

Al's eyes went wide. 'Good Lord! Athena Sapera? Now, there's a blast from the past!'

'Who is she?'

'A very old friend. Rhino lady. Read it out – and follow me.'

And so Beck followed Al into the living room, reading the rest of the letter line by line.

Chapter 3

Al searched around in the cupboard where he kept their old photo albums, while Beck continued.

'*I worked with your parents and your uncle in Africa for many years.*'

Beck paused and glanced at his uncle, who still had his head buried in the cupboard. 'True?' he asked.

'True.' Al's voice was slightly muffled. 'Keep going.'

'Hmm,' Beck muttered. The last time he met someone who'd worked with his parents, the man had been trying to kill him – an amateur assassin rather than a professional, but it had come to the same thing. As far as Beck was concerned, being an old parental friend did not necessarily mean anything. But he supposed he had to trust his parents' taste in friends at some point. They couldn't all have been bad.

'*I have been reading all about your adventures. You clearly take after your parents! They would be so proud of you—*'

'Got it.' Al dumped a heavy photo album down on the table and opened it at a page halfway through.

The first thing Beck saw was the rhinoceros, because it took up most of the picture. It was the size of a small car, armour-plated with folds of thick, dark leathery skin. He assumed it was sedated because it was lying down with its head between its front feet, like a very big dog stretched out in front of the fire.

On one side of the picture was his mother, just walking into the frame. Crouched down by the rhino's head, apparently checking its eyes, was another woman. She wore shorts and a checked shirt and a sun hat. Dark curly hair spilled out from under the brim. Her face was angled towards the camera, as if she had just noticed that her picture was being taken.

Al tapped her face with a finger and Beck

understood. This was Athena. He carried on reading.

'*I will shortly be returning to South Africa to continue my work with the rhinos in the Kruger National Park. You have probably heard of that . . .*'

Beck *had* heard of it. He knew that it was a large game reserve in South Africa – large, as in the size of a small country.

'*I wondered if you would like to come too. I am sure you find all your new fame very boring . . .*'

Beck pulled a wry smile. She was dead right there. It had been fine, until his scrape in Australia. Then the media had finally got hold of the fact that there was this boy who kept surviving – that was how the headline had described him. Since then he had been interviewed in print and on TV and on the web. He tried to use the fame wisely – he tried to push the Green Force message and say things that ought to be said. But yes, after a while it got boring. Always the same questions, always the same answers. And always the same closing line: 'So, Beck, what are you up to next?' The honest answer to that was always: 'Staying alive.'

He read on: '*. . . but I always say, if you've got it,*

13

use it. You would be the perfect face for a Green Force video highlighting the issue of rhino poaching. These wonderful animals are on the brink of extinction. There are only a few thousand white rhinos left, and black rhinos are down to a few hundred. If we don't change this now, then we never will.'

Beck scanned ahead. 'And then there's some stats about poaching . . .' He whistled. 'Four hundred and twenty-eight rhinos known to be killed in the first six months of 2013. That's, um . . .'

'Over seventy a month,' Al said grimly. 'More than two a day.'

'So anyway, she finishes: *I hope this is of interest to you. Please email me at . . .'* Beck raised his eyes to his uncle, who was looking thoughtful. 'So, what do you think?'

'What do *you* think?'

Beck thought that he could really do without having someone out to kill him. But two rhinos a day illegally killed . . . If there were only a few thousand of the creatures left, at that rate it really wouldn't be long before they disappeared for ever. He hated being in the limelight, but as Athena said, if you've got it, use it. If his fame could help . . .

'I want to do it.'

'Of course you do. And it doesn't occur to you for one second that going abroad on your own with Lumos on your tail would be the stupidest thing you could possibly do right now . . .'

'Why should Lumos know?' Beck asked. 'We don't have to tell anyone. I won't announce my holiday plans on PlaceSpace. I can just go, make the video, and be back before Lumos realizes I've gone.'

Al's eyes narrowed in thought. 'You know, that's not a bad idea. OK. Email her back and tell her you're coming.' He gave Beck a nudge. 'But *don't* tell her I'm coming with you. Let's surprise the lady.'

'You want to come too?' Beck said in surprise.

'Of course. And this time I'm staying with you every step of the way. Things go wrong when you're out on your own!'

Chapter 4

Beck and Al wheeled their cases into the arrivals hall of Johannesburg International Airport, and Beck scanned the waiting crowd. He had studied a couple more pictures of Athena, so he would know her when he saw her.

Identification was made easy when she almost screamed, '*Al!*'

She pushed her way through the mass of people to greet them. 'You devil! You never said you were coming too! And you must be Beck . . . Hello!'

She was dressed pretty much as she had been in the first photo Al had found: checked shirt, long shorts – though her curly hair was now touched with grey at the temples. She had dark brown eyes and a smile that could have been seen from space.

'So good to see you both! How was the flight? You got here just in time – the airport workers are about to walk out on strike. Here, come this way.'

Beck was left trailing in their wake, pushing the luggage trolley while Athena and Al strolled along arm in arm. The crowd closed in around them and he had to swerve constantly to avoid bumping into the people coming towards him. At one point someone stumbled into him, and he was pushed sideways into the path of an oncoming group; he felt like a pinball caught between the paddles. But then at last he saw the exit ahead.

Stepping out of the airport was always the moment when Beck knew he had *arrived* in a foreign country. It was when he took his first breath of the country's air – air at its natural temperature, not recycled through the aircon. Air that had blown across different continents and oceans.

In this case, it was like stepping into the blast of a warm hairdryer that blew all over his body. The air of South Africa's late summer had been baked dry, with not a drop of moisture left in it. It was quite early in the morning, but the sun was already showing some muscle, and Beck quickly slipped on his sunglasses.

In the car park Athena led them over to a battered Jeep with the Green Force logo on the doors. They slung their bags in the back.

'Did you sleep much on the plane?' she asked.

'No,' Al grumbled. He always found it hard to sleep on plane flights.

'Just fine, thanks!' Beck said with a smile.

A great thing about flying to South Africa was that even though it was a long way, it was almost due south of the UK. That meant there was very little jet lag – Johannesburg was only an hour ahead of London time. You could eat and sleep on the plane at the usual sort of times, and you arrived feeling just fine.

Most of the flight had been through the night. And Beck had loved staring down at the vast continent, miles beneath him, speckled with the occasional flicker of what could only be fires, oddly visible from 30,000 feet.

They set off down a wide, three-lane highway into the hectic Johannesburg traffic. As they pulled away from the airport, Athena said it would be about a half-hour's drive to where she lived when she was in town. They could spend the day and night there, to recover from the trip. Then, the following day, they would head off to the Kruger National Park so that Beck could make the video.

Very soon he could see the skyscrapers of Johannesburg rising up on the horizon. All around them on the highway, brand-new, modern Land Cruisers rubbed shoulders with battered old crates that looked like they would fall apart if you sneezed. It was the first reminder that South Africa was a peculiar country; one where the developed world and the developing world co-existed, side by side. That strange blend of wealth and poverty.

Chapter 5

They didn't talk much: Al was half asleep and Athena preferred to concentrate on driving – something Beck was very grateful for. The highway took them round the city, which passed by on their right. Eventually a sign told him that they were almost at Soweto.

'Almost there,' Athena said. 'In fact, Beck, it's not so far from where I first met your parents. We were all working in Soweto then.'

'There's rhinos in Soweto?' Beck asked in surprise. As he understood it, Soweto was a town-ship, a suburb of Johannesburg, not somewhere you would find wildlife. You found people there – hundreds of thousands of them, mostly living in shanty towns of corrugated iron and huts.

Al chuckled sleepily. 'They were jacks-of-all-trades,' he said. 'They did everything.'

'Al's right. Your father was the one who got involved with Green Force because of its wildlife work. Your mother was the humanitarian. She couldn't bear to see suffering and poverty when there were people all around with so much to give. In fact, I say I met your parents in Soweto – but that is also where they met each other!'

Book took a moment to absorb that fact. He hadn't known . . . He *had* known, of course, that his parents must have met, once. Just like there had been a time when he didn't exist, there must have been a time when they didn't know each other.

'Could we go there? Could we see it?' he asked suddenly.

Athena smiled. 'I'm not sure I know the exact place . . .'

'Could we just see the township?'

'Of course. If that's all right with you, Al?' Athena glanced across; he was still only half awake, but he shrugged. 'Very well. I know some people . . . Green Force have an outpost there. I'm not sure if they knew your parents, but they'll be very glad to see you.'

She smiled at Beck in the rear-view mirror. 'It was such a surprise when you got in touch! But you sounded so like your father in your letter. You had a good idea, you were determined to make it work—'

'Hey, wait – *what*?' Beck sat up, alert. 'I didn't get in touch. *You* got in touch! You sent me a letter on my birthday.'

'I sent you . . .?' Athena's smile was baffled. 'No, you wrote to me, remember? You had read about me in the Green Force newsletter and you thought maybe you could front a video campaign, since rhino poaching was so important to your parents . . .'

By now Beck and Al were looking very confused. Al turned round in his seat to frown back at Beck, and Beck shrugged to indicated that he had no idea what was going on.

'Hang on . . . Beck had his backpack beside him. He rummaged around and pulled out the letter Athena had sent. He tugged it out of its envelope, unfolded it and passed it to Al, who held it so that

Athena could look at it and still drive.

Her eyes went wide. 'That's not my hand-writing . . .' She scanned it quickly, all the way to the last line. 'And not my email address either.'

For a while there was silence in the car as each of them tried to work this out.

'Al,' Athena said eventually, in a quiet, determined voice, 'my bag is by your feet. Beck's letter is in the front pocket. Could you get it out . . . ?'

Al did as she asked. There was silence again, until he passed the letter back to Beck to read. It began, *Dear Athena, I don't know if you remember me . . .* and it was signed, *Beck Granger*.

'Same handwriting,' Beck murmured. 'And also not my email address.' Then, more loudly, 'So how did we all get to be here? If you and I were both emailing the wrong address—'

'Then whoever received those emails was passing them on to the right person – but in the meantime they were finding out all our plans,' Al said grimly. He twisted round to look at Beck again. 'You've been lured here, Beck. I wonder who it could be . . .'

Beck groaned and let his head fall back. He could only think of one answer, and he knew that Al was thinking the same thing.

Lumos.

Chapter 6

Athena pulled the car over into the shade of some trees and stopped. Wrapped up in the mystery of the letters, Beck hadn't noticed that they had left the highway.

She turned to face both of them. 'Al, what is going on?'

Al and Beck glanced at each other. Where to start . . . ?

Athena had heard about Beck's exploits – but they had never said anything in public about Lumos. So she didn't know anything about the threat from them.

'Long story,' said Al. 'Let's just say we've made enemies. Old enemies of Green Force who have decided to concentrate their attention on Beck.'

'And you think you're here because of them?'

'That is exactly what I think.'

Athena tapped the steering wheel in thought. 'So they know everything that was in the emails . . .'

'Yes. Athena, take us straight back to the airport, please. Beck is getting on the next plane out of this country, and I don't care where it's going.'

'I want to stay,' Beck said.

'And I don't care what you want.'

'We've got a job to do,' he insisted. 'Mum and Dad wouldn't have been scared off so easily, would they?'

'Your mum and dad's first priority would have been to keep you alive, and that's what I intend to do.' Beck opened his mouth again, and Al jabbed an angry finger at him. 'No! I'm putting my foot down. Athena, the airport, if you please.'

She was silent for a couple of moments. 'The airport will be closed by now,' she said with surprising calm. 'Remember I said you got in just before the strike? There'll be a backlog of flights already. You won't get out of the country that way for a couple of days at least.'

Al thumped the side of the car in frustration, but

Athena smiled. 'You want to stay one step ahead of them? Let's go on to the township. They don't know we've been discussing that. It wasn't in the emails. Beck can look around, and maybe you'll have a chance to decide what to do in peace.'

Beck saw a barrier ahead as the Jeep nosed down a lane. It was a makeshift arrangement of a pole and some oil drums. The large men standing in front of it scowled. They wore no uniforms but were very clearly toting guns – semi-automatic rifles slung over their shoulders. Their attitude was obvious – *We're on guard here and we're not letting you in*.

But Athena waved and sounded the horn in a series of *beeps* like a kind of code. The scowls broke into grins and the men stepped aside. One of them raised the barrier and waved the Jeep through.

Beck's first impression was of a sea of corrugated-iron roofs. Beneath this was a small city of shacks, cobbled together from concrete, iron sheeting, wire, bricks and the remains of old cars. Dirt tracks ran between them. The red soil of South Africa made Beck think of blood vessels – the paths of trampled mud were the veins and arteries of the shanty town.

But if the town was grubby, the people were certainly not. Every few paces, it seemed, there was a washing line draped with clothes and sheets hanging out to dry, all vibrantly coloured and patterned. Men, women, children – all carried themselves with confidence and dignity, but Beck also sensed they were reserved. They looked warily at the Jeep as it passed by, and they would smile or wave only when they saw the Green Force logo. Sometimes Athena waved back, or gave a friendly *beep*.

They pulled up on a hard-packed dirt space next to a cluster of shipping containers. The nearest was a cross between a butcher's and a barbecue. Inside, Beck caught a glimpse of red slabs of meat and piles of unidentifiable animal parts. Outside, they were being grilled on large metal drums and sold cheap to passers-by. They looked revolting, but the smell made Beck's mouth water.

Another container had several thick black telephone cables leading into it. It looked like it might be the local telephone exchange.

A third bore the Green Force logo.

Athena peered in. 'No one about,' she said. 'Let me give you the tour, then.'

Chapter 7

The three of them walked slowly down a crowded, narrow canyon between the shacks. Athena received a friendly nod from some of the locals, but most just watched the three white people impassively.

An open drain had been cut into the red soil and it glistened with stagnant water and waste. Beck was still in the comfortable shoes he had worn for the flight. He was forced to step from side to side over the drain, to let other people pass by. He wished he had changed into proper boots.

But compared to what these people faced, he thought to himself, spoiling a good pair of shoes wasn't such a big deal.

'No heating, no electricity, no running water,' said Athena.

As they walked, Beck looked around. Most of the huts had sheets instead of doors across the openings. Hardly any had glass in the windows.

'If a fire gets out of control, then it spreads immediately,' she went on, turning to Beck, 'and there's no way to fight it because there are no standpipes for the fire services. And there *will* be fires. It's warm enough now, but many people will die from the cold during the winter.'

In front of one of the shacks, a sheet was partially drawn back and a small child peered out. She – Beck was pretty sure it was a she – had eyes so large they seemed to take up most of her head, and her body was so thin that he wondered how she could stand.

He smiled his brightest smile. 'Hi.'

She vanished instantly, the sheet falling back over the doorway.

'Almost all the children suffer from malnutrition,' Athena continued. 'They don't develop properly; their bones don't grow. If they do eat, then there's a good chance the food is contaminated by rats or cockroaches, so there's dysentery and gastro-enteritis. Any food either comes straight back up or goes straight through and comes out as water at the other end. No running water means no proper toilets, no proper sewers or sanitation. So disease spreads like wildfire. Human waste gets into the water, and that leads to cholera. A bad attack of that will kill you in a few hours – you get dehydrated because all your body fluids come squirting out, in one direction or another.'

Beck could only stare. He felt like a gawping tourist, but he couldn't help it. And he felt anger growing inside him.

He was used to living rough and he had seen people who had very little. He had made many friends among them, and had learned a lot. But he had never witnessed poverty like this.

Some people were poor by Western standards, but they had everything they needed and they were happy. Some people were poor but, through hard work, could earn enough to keep going. But this kind of poor was something else. These people would never have enough and it didn't matter how hard they worked: they would stay poor because the system was unjust and it made sure they stayed that way.

Beck's anger grew. How dare anyone let people live like this? How *dare* they?

And this was what his mum had been fighting? He felt so proud of her . . .

A mother and two children crouched by an open fire, silently watching the three of them pass by. The little girl whimpered and shivered in her mother's arms. Her eyes were closed but her head twitched as though she had a fever, and she was scratching her leg, where the skin was rubbed almost raw.

Beck's anger came bursting out.

He strode forward and took the child's hand to stop her scratching. The mother didn't move. She just stared sullenly at him.

'She's got ticks,' Beck prompted.

There were three black dots embedded in the girl's skin. Beck was no stranger to ticks. The tiny insects buried their heads in the skin of their host and stayed there for days on end, drinking blood until they got bored or full. Their abdomens slowly swelled until they looked like black berries attached to the skin.

'I think she knows, Beck,' Athena said quietly.

She turned to the woman respectfully – '*Sawubona*, mother' – and received a grave nod in return.

'The girl has tick-bite fever. Very common. Not fatal, but it causes a temperature and headaches,' she told Beck.

Ticks also carried bacteria in their guts that could get into the victim's blood. Beck had heard of it but not seen it. Scratching a tick bite just made it worse – the skin was scraped raw and infection got in faster.

He was still angry. It was such a simple thing to cure.

'Right. I know how to get rid of them.'

Athena spoke in Zulu to the woman, who simply nodded again.

Beck looked around for inspiration and saw a pile of brushwood. He selected a small twig and held its tip in the fire until it began to smoulder.

Then he crouched down beside the girl and slowly held the smouldering tip out to touch the nearest tick. The girl's eyes half opened and she moaned when she saw him.

'Shh . . . It's OK . . . Shh . . .'

Being very careful not to touch her skin, Beck held

the hot tip against the black dot of the tick. Almost immediately it began to writhe and wriggle, and then it came loose. Beck quickly brushed it off her and took great pleasure in stamping the thing into the ground.

'OK, same again?' he asked cheerfully. He blew on the tip of the twig to heat it up, and turned his attention to the next tick on the girl's leg. It wasn't long before they'd all gone.

Athena spoke with the mother again. 'I'm telling her to bring the girl to the Green Force office. We'll give her something to help the fever.'

For the first time the mother showed some emotion. She looked at Beck, and said, 'Ngiyabonga.'

'It means "thank you",' Athena translated.

The little boy, who had been watching the procedure silently, suddenly flashed Beck a huge grin that took up most of his face. He thrust his arm forward. There was a tick just above the elbow.

Al laughed. 'I think you've found yourself a job, Beck.'

Chapter 8

The sun was high in the sky before Beck, Al and Athena returned to the Green Force office. Al was almost dead on his feet. Beck felt the comfortable glow inside that comes from knowing you've worked hard at something that was worth while.

'Hasn't anyone told them how to do this before?' he had asked as he removed what seemed like the thousandth tick from the hundredth kid.

'They probably have. Problem is, they always know the ticks will come back. It goes with the territory.'

Beck ground his teeth in frustration. He had always pictured his parents as warriors against the evil forces that wanted to ruin whole areas of the planet and drive animals into extinction, all because of greed. They had died doing battle, but they hadn't been defeated. It had been proof of how successful they were. Evil had felt threatened by them and it had lashed back the only way it knew how.

Maybe he could do just as much good working somewhere like this, helping people who were helpless.

He cocked one eye at the ramshackle shelters that people called home. He had built a few shelters out of less than these guys had. But then, he had only needed to stay alive for a night or two. He had never had to live in one. They had never been his home.

Maybe he could help out there too – show them how to make the shelters better, more wind- and waterproof . . .

As they approached the Jeep, Al turned to Beck. 'You've been brilliant, but please can we now get some sleep?' he begged.

Beck smiled, and turned round. A small crowd, mostly children, had silently followed them all the way down the alley. He waved at them, saying, 'Got to go. I'll be back!'

The solemn faces split into big smiles, and they waved enthusiastically. Beck grinned back. He gave a final wave and turned towards the Jeep.

An engine roared and another Jeep, black, modern and shiny, skidded to a halt next to them. Its tyres sent a cloud of red dust billowing up into the air around them.

Beck coughed, and suddenly his eyes were streaming. 'What the—?'

And then a tall, burly man emerged through the dust. He had a shock of grizzled hair that had once been dark, and muscular shoulders that strained at the fabric of his shirt. His jaw was set and determined as he wrapped his arms around Beck, lifted him up and hurled him towards the Jeep.

It was like being attacked by an agile silverback gorilla. Beck fell against the side of the vehicle, still too stunned to react. The man grabbed him by the scruff of his neck and the belt of his trousers, and pushed him through the open back door into the dark, cool interior. Beck blinked with streaming eyes and saw a face he had never thought he would see again. It belonged to a skinny blond boy a couple of years older than him, who had grabbed him by the arm.

James Blake. The boy who had tried to kill him once before . . .

Chapter 9

Beck swung a fist at James and wriggled out of his grasp. He reversed as fast as he could out of the Jeep, straight into the arms of the Silverback guy.

'No way, kid—' the man began.

Then he suddenly vanished as Al, in an astonishing blur of movement, brought him down in a charging rugby tackle. The two men sprawled on the red dirt in a winded heap. Beck and Athena ran forward to help Al up. The man who had attacked Beck tried to get to his feet, and then disappeared again amongst a mob of shouting, angry African children. The small crowd that had followed Beck set about him like a swarm of insects, kicking him, hitting him, pelting him with stones and mud.

'Come on,' Athena said, and she dragged Al and Beck back towards her car.

Beck took one last look at the black Jeep, its back door hanging open. James must still be in there, nursing his wounds.

Athena slammed Beck's door shut and clambered into the driver's seat. The engine roared and they surged away, leaving in their wake a cloud of red dust that soon obscured their view.

Al's chest heaved. 'Who the *blue blazes* was that?' he gasped.

'It was James,' Beck said. He inspected the hand with which he'd hit the other boy. It still hurt. 'James Blake. He was in that Jeep.'

Al stared at him with eyes like saucers as they sped along the track, rocking from side to side. 'James? Our friendly teenage psychopath James? James-who's-meant-to-be-dead James?'

Beck nodded.

Al swore and thumped the upholstery. 'That does it. This whole thing is one big Lumos trap. James failed once, so he'll try again and again, and each time he'll try harder. You need to keep on being lucky

41

over and over again to stay alive. He only needs to get lucky once to kill you. So we leave now, *today*.'

The Jeep slowed down a little to negotiate the potholes. Beck glanced behind them, but there was no sign of pursuit.

'I've already told you,' Athena said calmly. 'The airport is closed. Where do you suggest?'

'We go . . .' Al waved his hands in frustration. 'Somewhere! Just drive into the interior! Somewhere . . . anywhere they won't be expecting us to go!'

'What, like the townships?' Beck asked. 'Look, James failed – he won't have another plan immediately. He'll have to think about it. We should go ahead to the rhino reserve.'

'Which is exactly where James *knows* you'll be going,' Al pointed out.

'And we'll be surrounded by Green Force people,' said Beck. 'You know – anti-poaching rangers with big guns. And they'll know everyone, so any stranger will stand out like a sore thumb.'

Al's lips pursed thoughtfully. It looked like Beck's words had hit home.

'And remember,' Athena told him, 'the whole point

of you being here was so that Beck could make an advert to front the campaign.'

'Yes, but now we know that was Lumos's idea!'

'It doesn't matter whose idea it was . . .' For the first time Athena lost a little of her usual calm. Her anger and passion for the cause began to show through. 'It's still a critical one. This is so important, Al. So important! We are desperate for any help we can get. So what if this Lumos has accidentally helped us . . .'

Beck sensed that his uncle was weakening – though Al had one last stab at talking some sense into his nephew.

'There are still plenty of opportunities for Lumos to have another try,' he pointed out. 'If I remember correctly, it must be a seven- or eight-hour drive to the Kruger National Park. That's a lot of ground to cross. They could have men and guns strung out all along the way. They could strike at any time.'

Athena smiled. 'I think we can get there quicker than that, and I have a plan to make sure that Lumos won't have any chance at all.'

Chapter 10

The helicopter was cramped and noisy. Beck, Al, Athena and their luggage were crammed into the back, in a space not much larger than the inside of a saloon car.

But it was fast.

Athena had driven Beck and Al north to Pretoria, and then they had transferred to this helicopter, the property of Green Force. Athena had called ahead, so it was waiting for them, engine running. They had met the pilot, and another man who wore the faded khaki safari suit and sun hat of a park ranger.

Beck looked out of the window and saw low, rolling hills and grassland that flashed past beneath them. They had flown through the Drakensberg mountain range, the highest in Africa. It was torn and twisted land, pushed up by volcanoes millions of years ago, with some peaks over 3,000 metres high. And now they were flying low over the veld – rolling savannah that was home to all Africa's big game animals. Rhinos and elephants. Lions and leopards.

It was late in the day by now. The sun was starting to think about setting, and the shadows of trees and animals stretched out in front of them. The helicopter's own shadow looked like a giant insect running across the landscape. It leaped up and down as the ground rose and fell. A herd of zebra broke into a gallop for a few hundred metres, spooked by the roar of the flying object above them.

'We are under siege,' said a solemn voice in Beck's ears. Everyone wore headphones, so that they could communicate over the racket of the engine. The ranger, whose name was Bongani Peterson, had twisted round in the co-pilot's seat to talk to them. He was a tall Zulu man with hair that was starting to go grey at the temples.

'We have used the army, we have helicopter patrols, we have even started using drones to keep a lookout,' Bongani went on. 'But still the enemy comes.'

Beck and Al listened intently to the words of a man who spent his life in the front line of a battle that cost lives – not just rhino lives but human ones too. Rhino poachers knew the harsh penalties that awaited them if they were caught, and they would not hesitate to kill any ranger who found them.

'Where do they come from?' Beck asked.

Bongani pointed eastwards, ahead of them. 'Usually, over the border from Mozambique. The border is over two hundred miles long – difficult to police. And the park covers more than two million hectares. That is the size of Israel! They come in small groups, no more than four or five, and once they are here they can just disappear.'

'But four or five guys couldn't carry away a whole dead rhino – could they?' Beck was baffled.

'They don't want the whole rhino.' Bongani tapped his nose. 'They want just one bit – the horn. Unfortunately rhinos don't like parting with their horns, and so they have to kill them to get at it. The horn is worth more than gold on the black market. You hear all sorts of rubbish spoken about it. People think it is some kind of magical medicine – but, Beck, the horn is made of keratin! That's the same as your fingernails! If people think it's medicine, they might just as well put their fingernails in their tea and drink that.'

Beck pulled a face at the thought of fingernail tea. 'I hope it makes them really ill.'

Bongani's face broke into a grin. 'It does now! We're trialling a scheme where we inject the rhino's horn with pink dye. It doesn't get into the blood-stream so it won't harm the rhino – but any human who consumes it will suffer severe nausea and cramps. And because the horn is pink – which the rhinos don't mind; they're colour-blind – hopefully the poachers should be warned off killing that animal in the first place.'

Beck laughed. 'That's a neat idea.'

Bongani's smile faded and he shrugged. 'We hope so. But it's a never-ending battle. We can't inject dye into every single horn of every single rhino – and sooner or later the poachers, or the people they sell the horns on to, will work out how to bleach the dye out again. That means it will no longer appear pink – but the poison will still be there to

make people ill. You have to remember, Beck: people are stupid, and greedy, and wicked – and so the
rhinos die.'

The pilot's voice broke into the conversation.

'Ten more minutes and we're there.'

Chapter 11

The sun was on the horizon when the helicopter touched down amidst a cloud of swirling dust. It stayed on the ground just long enough for everyone to pile out with their luggage. Then it took off again while they hurried over to the lodge.

This was Green Force's local headquarters. It was a working building, not the kind of place where rich tourists were accommodated. No Jacuzzi or sun deck here. It was a low wooden bungalow, raised on stilts as a precaution against insects and snakes. The roof was dry thatch and the windows were unglazed.

Until you saw the other rangers, or the vehicles parked out front, the satellite dish at one end was the only reminder that you were still in the twenty-first century.

The wooden steps and veranda led straight into the lodge's main room. It was furnished with cane chairs, and ceiling fans lazily circulated the air around the wide open space. An African girl Beck's age sat at a table, hunched over a laptop. She lifted her head long enough to smile at them, but then her attention went back to the screen while she scribbled notes on a pad.

'Samora,' Bongani started to say, 'this is—'

'She's on the move again,' Samora whispered, waving him to silence.

Bongani cocked an eyebrow at Beck and Al and Athena, but he looked amused. They walked over to the table to see what was absorbing the girl's interest.

It meant nothing to Beck. The screen showed a bunch of wiggling lines superimposed over a map. A dot on the screen was slowly moving along one of them. A cluster of digits next to it showed what Beck presumed were its latitude and longitude. Every now and then a digit would change as the dot's position shifted.

Bongani put a hand on Samora's shoulder and

she squeezed it. They were both obviously pleased with whatever was being shown on the screen. Beck wondered why they were all being so quiet; whatever the computer showed, it couldn't exactly hear them, could it?

'What is it?' he asked softly.

'She's an elephant,' Samora said, not looking up. 'She was raised by humans but we released her into the wild. Now she's pregnant and . . . see the routes she's following?' She indicated the lines on screen. 'Those are the usual migration routes. We can see she's falling into the same behaviour patterns as the rest of the herd.' She flashed Beck a brilliant smile and he could sense her happiness. 'It means they've accepted her.'

Bongani made the introductions. 'Samora, sweetheart, this is Beck and Al. Athena you know. Samora is my daughter . . .'

'So, do you know all about rhinos too?' Beck asked on an impulse. He hadn't realized that there would be someone his own age here; he would be glad of the company, he thought.

Samora smiled. 'A little.'

Bongani rolled his eyes. 'What doesn't she know? Come on, you can catch up later. You'll both maybe want a lie down before we eat . . .'

Chapter 12

After breakfast the next day Beck sat on the veranda of the lodge and looked out at the park. Trees and shrubs stretched out to the horizon in every direction like a thin veil across the ancient land.

This, he thought, *this* was Africa – a land rich in majesty and beauty. The shanty town from yesterday was like a cancer in a healthy body. Cancer happens when a body's natural mechanisms go wrong. The shanty town was a place where Africa, which could be so great with all its riches and its vibrant people, turned in on itself instead.

Beck wanted to be like a doctor, helping it to right itself again. Somehow . . .

The previous evening, after an early supper, Beck had fallen asleep with his mind full of the wild. The scent of the dry grass, and the endless song of insects and the occasional animal cry in the distance. The next morning he woke early, full of anticipation – though he had a strange fluttery feeling in the pit of his stomach, half excitement, half fear.

He wandered out onto the lodge's veranda and looked across the game park.

Now that he was viewing it at ground level, rather than from the air, he finally felt like he had properly arrived in Africa.

Twenty metres away stood a wooden sign, aimed at any visitors who might not be used to the park:

DO NOT WEAR BRIGHT CLOTHES –

IT UPSETS THE ELEPHANTS

Beck thought of the sign outside his own house back in London – RESIDENTS' PARKING ONLY – and smiled to himself. He preferred this one. He would like to live in a place where elephants might come wandering by.

Beck and Al, who were no rookies to life in the wild, had brought the right clothes with them, so the elephants had nothing to worry about. They had hats with wide, floppy brims to shade their eyes and protect their brains from the sun. On their feet were lightweight, sturdy safari boots, which cushioned their soles and supported their ankles on rough ground. Their shirts and trousers were made of tough ripstop material, loose enough to let the air circulate next to their skin; the dull greens and browns looked almost like camouflage.

Beck felt comforted by the thought that he could just blend into the background of the park if he had to.

He heard footsteps on the decking, and Samora came to sit down beside him.

'Morning!' She waved a hand out at the park. 'So, what do you think?'

'It's beautiful,' he said sincerely.

'Dad said you're going to make a video about rhinos?'

'That's right. On the way here he was telling us about the poaching.'

A cloud passed over Samora's smiling face. 'Bad people. Bad, desperate people. I'm learning about conservation – I'm going to be a ranger when I'm older.'

Bongani and Athena had come out of the lodge too. Athena had a camera bag slung over her shoulder and Bongani was carrying a tripod. They walked down the steps to set up the tripod on the dusty ground.

'Samora is already a veteran at taking DNA samples,' Bongani said.

'DNA?' Beck asked in surprise. Surely she didn't need to be a genetic scientist in order to become a ranger . . .

'We take the DNA of dead rhinos that we find and send it off to Johannesburg,' Samora explained. 'It goes into a database so that it can be matched against any products that come onto the market. And we collect the bullet cases for evidence too.' Her smile died away. 'Did Dad tell you about the mother and baby we found yesterday?'

Beck shook his head.

Her eyes went a little distant as she remembered. 'We knew something was wrong because we saw the vultures circling. They always do that above dead animals – it's usually the first sign that something is wrong. So we went looking. The rhinos must have been killed four or five days earlier. First we found the baby. The vultures and hyenas had stripped it down to its bones.' She paused.

'The poachers must have shot it first – they were probably aiming for the mother and missed. They would have left the child because the horn was too small. So, one less rhino for absolutely nothing. The mother was lying a few hundred metres away, with a huge hole where her horn used to be. There is nothing more disgusting than that hole – it's dark and ugly, full of thick black blood and buzzing flies.'

Samora's voice trembled for a moment. She paused, rubbed one eye with a finger, and continued more calmly, back under control.

'She must have run for her life when the baby was killed. She would have been in agony . . . there was a wound in her shoulder – they hit her at least once before killing her.' She was clearly struggling to contain her fury at the loss of these magnificent creatures' lives.

Beck felt it too. An anger that burned deep inside

him. He remembered Bongani's remark about finger-nails. Who were these people? How could they do this to those beautiful animals? And all for fingernail medicine . . .

'Perfect!' Athena said. 'Hold that thought!' She had clamped the camera onto the top of the tripod and swung it round to face Beck.

He blinked. 'What thought?'

'You're angry, aren't you?'

'Of course I'm angry!'

'Then that's the thought to hold. We need to hear it in your voice, see it in your eyes. You can start by telling the story that Samora just told you, while it's fresh in your mind. OK! Set, and . . . *go*!'

And so Beck told the story, calmly but passionately.

But as he finished his first bit of filming, he knew that the real story was only just beginning.

Chapter 13

'Pull over here, Al,' Samora said from the back seat.

The Jeep was bouncing along a track that led along a small ridge. Al obediently turned onto a packed dirt area where it was obvious a lot of other vehicles had stopped before.

He killed the engine, and Beck saw why Samora had chosen this spot.

The veld of the Kruger National Park stretched away in front of them. In the far distance, on the horizon, Beck could see the Drakensbergs, the mountain range they had flown over the day before.

From here he could look down a gentle slope towards a waterhole. It was a darker spot in the grasslands, surrounded by trampled mud from the feet of all the creatures that relied on it to stay alive.

A small herd of impala were clustered around it now, heads down to drink. They were sleek, graceful creatures, with horns that were thin and curved.

'I guess they're not endangered,' Beck said, looking down at the herd.

'No, they're safe. One and a half million at the last count,' Athena told him.

'Almost as many as the different camera shots you wanted when we were filming!' Beck joked.

Athena smiled. She had always been a perfectionist, and she knew that sometimes it could be a trial for those around her.

After they had done their initial filming with Beck, Athena had set off with Bongani in a Green Force Jeep to take additional shots for the ad. She had a few ideas for some landscapes and places where she could get close-ups of animals. Meanwhile Al had taken another Jeep to show Beck some more of the park from the ground. Samora had come along to keep them company, which Beck was grateful for.

Now he scanned the landscape to see what else he could pick out.

All was quiet for a few 'African' minutes, as Al

called them. Minutes that had no time to them. Maybe it had been five . . . maybe fifteen. All that mattered was the sense of stillness and calm. This was what Al, and Beck's parents, had always loved about Africa.

Beck spotted them first. A herd of elephants, maybe fifteen or twenty of all sizes, was plodding towards the waterhole to drink. He watched in awe. He knew people who lived in houses that were smaller than the herd leader. The impala guessed what the enormous animals wanted and decided to move on.

When Beck was little, Al had told him that African elephants were called that because their ears were the shape of Africa, and Indian elephants got their name because their ears were shaped like India. Al had enjoyed telling him stories like that, and Beck couldn't deny it: African elephants had the bigger ears, and they did look like a map of Africa. Sort of.

Three or four giraffes were wandering gracefully past, a few hundred metres beyond the elephants. Their necks swayed with the rhythm of their movement, and they almost seemed to float across the dry grass.

And then Samora gasped and clutched Beck's arm. 'Look!'

He followed her outstretched finger, and for a moment couldn't see what the excitement was.

And then he saw it, emerging from a group of bushes.

A magnificent, slow-moving rhino . . .

Chapter 14

It approached with total confidence. Steady, methodical, dignified.

Beck knew that rhinos were peaceful, vegetarian animals that wished no harm to anyone; but he also knew that they had very short tempers and could lash out at anything that irritated them.

This rhino moved like it knew its own strength. With all its weight behind it, the horn could do a lot of damage, and its body was armour-plated, so it feared nothing. No meat-eating animal would be stupid enough to attack a full-grown adult rhino. Probably the only creature that could have hurt it was an elephant, and why would an elephant want to?

No wonder this rhino moved along so calmly, at peace with the world.

Unfortunately, though, Beck knew that the reality was very different.

This was a world of poachers carrying high-powered rifles – something this magnificent creature would have no defence against. But there was no sign of any poacher today. Beck, Samora and Al were the only three humans around, and they were a hundred metres or so away at the top of a hill. The rhino was too short-sighted to spot them up there.

'It's a black,' Samora said reverently. 'They're so rare. At the last count there were three hundred and fifty of them in the park. We are very lucky to be seeing it.'

The rhino was built like a mammalian tank. It was the height of a man and getting on for twice as long – Beck estimated about four metres from nose to tail. Its head moved slowly from side to side as it peered out of tiny eyes set low on either side of its skull.

When its head moved, the mighty horn – the cause of all its troubles – reminded Beck of a gun-sight. As if the animal was constantly taking aim at anything that might dare to trouble it.

Nothing did. The rhino continued on its way.

'Doesn't really look black, does it?' Beck commented. The rhino was a darkish shade of grey, nothing more.

'It's just darker than a white rhino, that's all,' Samora told him.

'Which aren't white,' Al said with a smile.

Still looking through Al's binos, Samora added, 'White rhinos get their name from the Dutch word *wijd*, which means *wide*. They're really *wide* rhinos.'

Beck looked at Al.

'It's their mouths.' Al tapped his own. 'Wide and straight, unlike the black.'

Beck could see that the black rhino's mouth ended in a pointed snout.

'So beautiful,' Samora murmured. Beck agreed.

They watched until the rhino had dwindled to a dot that shimmered in the heat. Then Al fired up the engine again and pulled away.

The track dipped down into a shallow valley. The ground rose up on either side, and for a moment they no longer had the wonderful views out to the horizon. A herd of grazing zebra broke into a trot to get away from the vehicle. They were just playing it safe and avoiding potential danger.

They drove on through a group of trees and bushes, curving around a sharp incline so that they couldn't see more than twenty metres ahead. Al came round the corner and then braked. Hard.

Standing in the middle of the road, facing them, was another rhino.

Judging from Samora's description earlier, this one had to be a white rhino, Beck guessed. Its hide was a pale grey, and its mouth was set in an angry line.

More importantly, it was massive – about a quarter as long again as the black rhino they had seen earlier, and taller too. It filled the road so that there was no way past it. Its head was close to the ground, ears laid back. The rhino lowered its head and scraped its horn along the ground.

No one moved for a few seconds, then Al put his hand on the gearstick, saying, 'I'll reverse—'

Samora grabbed his arm. 'No,' she said. There was a strange tone in her voice. 'Just turn the engine off.'

'Off?'

'Off.'

Al killed the engine with an abrupt twist of the keys.

In the sudden silence they could hear the rhino's breath – abrupt puffs of air from a pair of massive bellows.

'This beast can run faster than you can ever accelerate' – Samora spoke slowly – 'and it's showing all the signs of wanting to charge us.'

Chapter 15

The rhino lowered its head and rubbed its horn along the ground. Then it looked up again and stared at them. Beck stared back, then quickly looked away. Some animals take a direct stare as a challenge. He wasn't going to risk provoking it.

He wondered what it would be like if it charged. Was the Jeep stronger than it looked? Would it stand up to the creature's massive weight? Or would it just crumple like tin foil?

He really, really wished Samora had let Al keep the engine running. But he understood that if the noise of the Jeep was one of the things angering the rhino, then their best chance was to turn it off.

'Lions roar to warn attackers off,' Samora said

quietly. She hadn't taken her eyes off the rhino. 'Rhinos use body language.'

The rhino lowered its head again and let out a massive huff through its nostrils. Its breath blew a small cloud of dust up off the track.

Samora continued, 'Like that – they blow out through their noses, they rub their horn . . .'

'Why's this one angry?' Beck asked.

'Could be territory – he thinks this road belongs to him. Or it could just be a bad day at the office.'

Beck smiled weakly at the joke. He was still filing the information away at the back of his mind. His expertise was survival – he knew how to live off the land and stay alive long enough to get from A to B. He knew how to find food, how to build shelters – but sooner or later any survivor was likely to come into contact with wildlife, and it was important to know what to do then too.

He smiled, thinking to himself, *In cases like this, the best answer is to stay away*.

The rhino tossed its head as if trying to shake something off the tip of its horn. Then it slowly turned and ambled away into the bushes. Beck blew out a sigh of relief, almost as strong as the rhino's final *huff*.

'Please can I turn the engine on again?' Al asked.

'Sure.' Samora smiled weakly. 'Before it changes its mind.'

They had been out all day and Beck was looking forward to getting out of the Jeep. There were good roads in the park, but they had stayed off them, and Al's answer to the potholes was to just keep going and pretend they weren't there. The majesty of the African landscape was some compensation for the uncomfortable ride, but Beck was looking forward to enjoying the views from the veranda of the lodge.

The colours of the day were slowly turning to yellow and red. Beck knew it would get dark very fast here. The closer you were to the equator, the more quickly the sun rose and fell. Here, in the corner of South Africa, they were much nearer to the equator than London is. Al estimated that they were maybe half an hour from the lodge.

And then Beck noticed the vultures.

It was movement at the corner of his eye. Black

specks against the blue sky, wheeling high above the veld.

He glanced up at them.

They were ugly, graceless birds and he didn't think much of them. On the ground, their ragged black feathers and bent necks made them look like old men going to a funeral in tattered old suits. Soaring through the air, they appeared menacing, as if waiting to be beckoned down to earth by the stench of death.

'Remember what you said about vultures being the first sign that something is wrong . . .?' Beck spoke over the noise of the bumping Jeep. 'Well, look up there . . .'

Chapter 16

Samora and Al didn't need to say anything. Al turned the wheel and the Jeep bounced off the track and across the grass towards the spot where the vultures were circling.

'Did I mention that vultures have their own problems with the poachers?' Samora asked.

'Go on . . .' said Beck.

'Poacher kills rhino, vultures start to circle, rangers detect dead rhino – so some poachers are now planting poison in the rhino carcasses to kill the vultures, so they won't circle, so no one will see them. During the breeding season, one dead rhino might be eaten by six hundred vultures. But if you kill the adults, then their chicks will die too because there is no one to feed them – which means one dead rhino equals twelve hundred dead birds.'

Beck shook his head. 'It makes you feel sick, doesn't it? It's just such a waste.' He looked back up to the sky.

Five or six vultures were circling above a group of bushes. They soared on wide, dark wings, comfortably riding the currents of hot air. One of them dropped down amongst the vegetation, which meant there must be clear ground in there somewhere.

Al drove three-quarters of the way round the scrub before he found a way in. The Jeep nosed its way through, and stopped.

A rhino was lying on its side and Beck's heart plummeted. Then he saw the horn on its nose. It was still intact. This rhino hadn't fallen victim to the poachers.

As they drew closer, Beck could see its sides moving up and down. It was alive, so the vultures hadn't plucked up the courage to start eating it yet. They weren't killer birds – they preferred to wait until a dead meal was provided for them.

Three or four of them had landed nearby and were quietly waiting. They spread their wings and flapped clumsily up and away as the Jeep came closer.

Al reached for the keys.

'Wait a moment . . .' Beck said. He climbed up on his seat and peered around. 'It's always worth making sure there's no other rhino nearby that might get mad. It only takes a second to check, but it can cost you your backside if you rush in and get caught out!' He gave a wry smile as Al turned off the engine and they climbed out.

The rhino was a female. The one eye they could see was half open and her ears twitched to shake the flies off. A thick river of drool ran down her leathery lips to the ground. The *whoosh* of breath in her nostrils, one at either end of her wide, straight mouth, sounded like it came from a machine rather than a living creature.

They approached cautiously, eyes peeled for anything that might be amiss.

Samora gently laid a hand on the rhino, but she didn't move. 'I don't think she's been shot,' she said. 'She's just ill.'

Beck remembered what poachers had started doing to the vultures. 'Has she been poisoned?'

'I don't think so. They tend to do that to the bodies after they're dead. She needs a vet. Is there a radio in the Jeep?'

'I didn't see one,' Al said grimly, but he hurried back to check. It only took a few moments. 'No, there isn't,' he confirmed.

'There'll be someone at the lodge who will know what to do,' Samora told him.

'Then that's where we'll go now. Back in, you two—'

'I'd like to stay.'

Al raised his eyebrows. 'No offence, Samora, you know this land better than we do – but is it safe? I'm thinking lions, hyenas . . .'

'Then you'd better hurry,' she said simply.

Al didn't argue. The bush was like Samora's second home. 'OK. Beck, let's get going—'

'No,' Beck said. 'I'm staying too.'

He and Al locked eyes. Beck knew that this time his uncle was thinking of deadlier predators than lions and hyenas.

He wasn't quite sure what Samora could do for the rhino, but if there was any chance of helping, he wanted to be there too.

'They can't know we're here, Al,' he said quietly. Only Al would have known who 'they' were. 'And you don't want to leave Samora alone, do you?' he went on quickly. 'You could stay, only I can't drive,' he added cheekily.

Finally Al nodded and climbed into the driver's seat. 'I'll be about an hour, depending on how quickly they react at the lodge.'

The Jeep reversed out of the bushes, and Beck and Samora were left alone with the dying animal.

Chapter 17

Beck reached out to touch the rhino for the first time.

He did it reverently, because who would want any old stranger just coming up and pawing them? The hide under his fingertips felt like warm, dry mud. It was hard to believe it belonged to a living animal.

'Rub under her throat,' Samora said. 'They like that.'

Beck did as he was told. Unlike the armour-plated hide, the thin skin of the throat felt as soft as a baby's. He had a feeling of awed privilege at being allowed to bring some kind of comfort, however small, to this massive creature. Stupidly, he and Samora had left their water bottles in the Jeep; otherwise they could have given some to the rhino.

'Can you tell what's wrong with her?'

Samora was moving slowly along the rhino's side, peering and poking her fingers into every nook and cranny in the skin.

'There are no wounds. She hasn't been shot. And they have no real predators apart from humans. It could be a bacterial infection – I don't like all that dribble coming out of her mouth.'

Beck thought back to a headline he had caught on the plane to Johannesburg. Al had been reading the in-flight magazine. 'Isn't there something called "rhinovirus"?'

Samora bit back a laugh, but couldn't hide a smile. 'Beck, that's just another name for the common cold in humans. Rhinos can't catch it!'

'Yeah, well. Figure that . . .' Beck felt himself blush, and they both chuckled.

He rubbed the rhino's throat again while Samora continued with her inspection. She drew back the thick lids and peered into the eyes.

'There's a few ticks here, but that's usual. Sometimes they can get trypanosomiasis from tsetse flies – it means they just slowly waste away. But we'd need a blood test to confirm that.'

Samora squatted back and gazed at the rhino with moist eyes. 'Or it could just be colic. A twisted bowel – her food can't travel through her properly, so it rots inside and poisons her.'

'What will the vet be able to do?'

'See if I'm right. If it's the trypanosomiasis, then we could clear it up with antibiotics. Or if it's the twisted bowel' – a corner of her mouth twitched – 'untwist it. That means you put your hand inside, and feel about, and remove the blockage – and everything comes right out, under pressure. And you know all about it then!'

She was trying to make light of it, and Beck smiled back, wincing. Then Samora's face was sad again. Beck knew that it was horrible for her: one of her beloved rhinos was slowly dying in front of her eyes and there was nothing she could do to help.

So as they waited for the vet, they did whatever they could to alleviate the rhino's sufferings. Beck kept rubbing the rhino's throat. Samora scratched the folds of skin around her ears. If these were the rhino's last hours, at least they could make them slightly more comfortable. The light was fading; the sun had already sunk down behind the surrounding bushes. Beck was pretty certain that this rhino wouldn't be seeing it come up again.

Abruptly the rhino let out a last snort of air through her nostrils. And that was it. Her sides simply stopped moving. Her eyelid stopped flickering and there was silence.

Samora bit a trembling lip and lowered her head. Beck reached out hesitantly, and put an arm round her shoulders. 'I'm so sorry,' he said. And Samora gripped his hand tightly and cried.

Beck's ears pricked up at the sound of an approaching engine. It was revving hard; the driver was obviously accelerating across the veld. 'Too late,' he murmured.

They both got to their feet and waited for Al and the lodge's vet to appear. But it wasn't a Green Force Jeep that burst through the bushes.

Beck's first thought was that James had found him again. Yet it wasn't the sleek black car with tinted windows that he remembered, either. It was a battered pick-up truck with a canvas roof. It lurched to a sudden halt in front of them.

It was hard to say who was more surprised – Samora and Beck, or the two men in the cab, staring out at them.

The driver leaped down and advanced towards them. He wore a battered, floppy bush hat, and carried a rifle with a long curving magazine. He barked what was obviously a question in a language Beck didn't understand.

The other man climbed down more slowly and came forward. He held his rifle at the ready, one finger tapping against the trigger guard. He was clearly trying to decide whether he should use the gun.

'Beck . . .' Samora said quietly, but Beck didn't need to be told who these people were.

He swallowed.

These were poachers.

Chapter 18

The two men spoke to each other quickly, and then the driver hurried back to the truck. He returned carrying a hacksaw and a brown sack.

Beck suddenly realized what he was going to do. 'No!'

He stepped in front of the rhino to block the man's path. The poacher simply gave him a shove that sent him flying. Samora threw herself at him and was knocked aside in the same way. By the time Beck picked himself up, the man had knelt down beside the dead rhino and was starting to saw at the base of the horn.

Even then Beck was prepared to try and stop him. But the second man shouted, 'Hey!' He had raised the rifle so that it pointed straight at Beck. And he didn't look like he would hesitate to squeeze the trigger.

And so the pair had no choice but to stand there while the man with the saw did his grisly work. Tears rolled down Samora's face as she watched the butchery, so they turned away – though they couldn't block out the brutal sound of the saw as the beautiful animal was desecrated by the poachers.

Within minutes the horn was off. Beck turned to see the gaping bloody hole where it had been. He felt sick inside, while beside him Samora was sobbing.

The man standing in front of them waved the barrel of his rifle in their faces and threw questions at them.

'*Quem é você? O que você está fazendo?*'

'*Nós estávamos tentando ajudar o rinoceronte,*' Samora answered. To Beck, she added, 'He wants to know who we are and what we're doing; I told him we were trying to help the rhino.'

'Where are they from?'

'Mozambique. That's Portuguese he's speaking.'

'Hey!' The man didn't like them talking to each

other in English. He waved the gun aggressively from one to the other, and asked more questions. Samora answered as calmly as she could, though her voice trembled.

It was hardly surprising, Beck thought, with a gun being pointed at them like that. It is a natural reaction to fear – the start of panic.

It wasn't the first time he had been held at gun-point, but that didn't make it any easier. His whole body was taut with nerves; the hairs on the back of his neck were standing up, alert.

Beck had a bad feeling about how this was going to end.

'Meh.' The man grunted in disgust and suddenly strode over to his friend.

Samora and Beck watched him go, and Beck's anger began to boil again when he saw the bloody mess of rhino horn in the poacher's hand.

'*Devemos matá-los*,' said the man with the gun. At that, Samora gasped and went rigid. '*Eles viram as nossas caras*.'

The colour drained from Samora's face as she translated for Beck's benefit. 'H-he said, "W-we should kill them. Th-they've seen our faces."'

'*Eu não estou nessa para matar crianças!*' the man carrying the rhino horn objected angrily.

Samora whispered her translation to Beck. 'He said, "I'm not in this to kill kids."'

Beck didn't reply. He had seen bad men fall out before.

The men continued to argue.

'If it looks like they're going to do it,' Beck whispered over his pounding heart, nodding to their left, 'run that way. I'll go this way . . .' He looked to the right.

Finally the one with the gun wheeled round towards them. The two friends braced themselves to flee, in a last desperate attempt to save their lives. But the man simply jerked the gun at the truck.

'In back,' he ordered abruptly. 'Boss decide.'

If Beck had found the Jeep uncomfortable, it was nothing compared to being thrown around in the back of a pick-up truck. Their feet and hands were bound with lengths of old rope that bit into their skin. It was dark outside now and they could barely see each other in the gloom beneath the canvas cover. And it was stiflingly hot.

There were no seats, just a rusting, dirty metal floor to perch on as the truck lurched its way across the veld. With their hands tied behind their backs it was almost impossible to hold onto anything. Just as they managed to lever themselves upright, the truck would hit another bump and they would fall over again.

Even so, Beck managed to shuffle himself over to the side of their bouncing prison. He lowered his head to the bottom of the canvas cover and tried to peer out underneath. He bit back a curse as another bump made his chin bang against the metal edge.

'What are you doing?' Samora asked. At first they had talked in whispers because it seemed right, but the pickup was so noisy that only loud voices could possibly have been heard by those in the front. Beck doubted their kidnappers were listening in.

'I want to see the stars,' he said. He rested his head against the metal and strained the one eye that he could get close to the gap. 'If I can see the stars, then I'll know which direction we're heading, and how far we go.'

'OK, that's smart, Beck Granger.' She paused. 'But my watch has GPS on it.'

Beck twisted round to face her. He could see only the faintest outlines in the dark, but he was pretty sure she was smiling.

'OK.' He shuffled over towards her.

Using Samora's watch wasn't easy. They had to sit back to back so that Beck could operate it by feel. Then he had to turn round very quickly and look at the watch face, which stayed lit for only twenty seconds at a time.

But eventually they worked out what Beck had already guessed.

They were being taken across the border, into Mozambique.

Chapter 19

There was very little they could do except wait.

They explored every inch of their small moving prison, but could find nothing to help them. All the men's tools and weapons must be carried in the cab.

Beck made his way all around the edge of the truck, where the canvas cover met the metal edge. The ties that held the cover in place were on the outside and he couldn't have got at them even if his hands had been free. The flap at the rear was secured with bolts on the outside.

Every so often Beck would check Samora's watch to get an idea of how far they had travelled. He mentally translated that figure into the length of the trek back – if they ever managed to escape.

No – they *would* escape; he was determined about that.

But there was no way they could escape from this truck. They could only wait until they reached their destination. He hoped it wouldn't be too far into Mozambique.

It was three hours before the truck came to a sudden stop that threw them both against the back of the cab. Artificial orange light showed through the canvas. There were several voices, all men's, talking in Portuguese. Then the cover was pulled back, the flap lowered, and their old friend with the gun was gesturing abruptly.

'*Sair!*'

Beck didn't need to speak Portuguese to realize that they were being told to get out. They shuffled over to the back of the truck, where they were dragged out and thrown to the ground. They managed to land on their feet, though Beck immediately stumbled as pins and needles took hold. He hadn't been able to stand since they were captured, and the ropes had cut off his circulation.

The truck had stopped in a small compound. There were low buildings on all sides, some inhabited, some just storage barns and outhouses. And there were far too many men for Beck's liking – he could see five, plus their kidnappers, without even moving his head. The more there were, the harder it would be to get away.

Several of them were engaged in a loud argument with their kidnappers.

Samora was standing next to him, looking equally wobbly. 'They want to know why they've brought two kids back with them,' she murmured, which Beck had already guessed.

One of the kidnappers held up the bag that contained the severed rhino horn, which seemed to calm the others down a little.

Then one man came over to them. There was a flash of steel as he pulled a knife from his belt and brandished it in front of them with a cruel smile. Beck felt his guts lurch inside him, but he gritted his teeth and tensed his body, ready to throw himself forward. If they were going to be stabbed instead of shot, he might as well go down fighting –

which could, in turn, allow Samora to make a break for it.

But the man just crouched down and slashed through the ropes that tied Samora's ankles together. Beck was next. Now they could walk properly, though their hands were still bound.

Beck hopped from one foot to the other to get the blood flowing again, before a shove in the small of his back sent him staggering towards one of the out-buildings. Like all the others, it was propped up off the ground to keep out any snakes or creepy crawlies.

Beck had one foot on the steps when a voice shouted, 'Hey!'

They were both pulled to a halt. The man with the knife reached behind Samora's back and grabbed her tied wrists. She winced as he pulled her hands up to have a look at her watch, before undoing the strap and releasing it.

'That's the taxi fare!' he said with a grin, holding it up.

Another man did the same with Beck's watch. Then a shove sent the pair on their way again. They turned to see the expensive new toy being passed around and shown off.

Beck was glad they hadn't left it on the GPS setting. He didn't want these people to know that their captives knew exactly where they were.

The inside of the hut was almost as dark as the truck had been. A sheet of plywood had been nailed across the window, and a narrow band of light slid in around the edges. He could see a battered wooden bed frame and a table and a couple of chairs. A final shove sent him and Samora stumbling inside and the door was pulled shut behind them. Beck heard the sound of a key turning in the lock. Then footsteps on the steps again. Then silence.

They looked at each other through the gloom. Their feet hadn't been tied again, but their hands were still bound.

'So we've lost the watch,' Samora said.

Beck shook his head. 'I memorized our location.'

Samora smiled, clearly dubious. *Of course you did, Beck Granger!* After all, it was only a fourteen-digit number of longitude and latitude. 'Did you really, Beck?' she asked.

Beck didn't reply. He was busy looking around the room.

'OK. Let's see what we've got, so that we can get out of this stinking place.'

Chapter 20

It didn't take long to explore the room and its contents. There were no useful tools – nothing that Beck immediately identified as being helpful. Even something like a knife or a fork might have come in handy.

He went over to the back of the room and studied the boards carefully – both on the floor and in the wall. Escaping out through the front wasn't going to work, because that was where all the men were. If they were going to get out at all, then it had to be at the back.

Beck crouched down and inspected the floorboards. They had been nailed rather than screwed down, and that made him feel hopeful. A nail just goes straight in, and what goes straight in can come straight out again.

There were gaps between the boards, and he reckoned there was just enough space below the hut for them to crawl out underneath. Maybe he could wedge something into the spaces and lever the boards up.

But first he and Samora had to get untied.

'Come and stand in the light,' he told her.

Samora came over to stand by the window, and Beck looked at the knots that bound her. Now that he could actually see them, he might have something to work with.

A real expert would have known how to fasten each hand individually, then bind them together so that there was no way they would ever came loose. But the guy who had tied them up was no expert. He had just wrapped the ends of the rope around each other and pulled them tight, over and over again.

The knots were still tight, but in theory, Beck should be able to work his hands loose eventually. Every time he flexed his wrists, the ropes would grow a little looser. The problem was, it would take hours, and in the meantime the rough strands would scrape the skin off his wrists.

'OK . . .' He turned round and they stood back to back so that his hands could get at her knots. He bit his lip in concentration as he felt his way. It would be easier to loosen Samora's knots for her, if he could only see them. But the rope was old and greasy, and it wasn't easy to get a purchase with just his finger-tips, fumbling behind his back.

'We need something to jam between the knots . . .'

If Beck could do that – let something else take the pressure – he could work the knots loose much quicker. He let his eyes wander around the hut again.

'That chair doesn't look too strong,' Samora suggested.

The wooden chair was a rickety relic from another age, the legs, seat and supports slotted together. Now, any one of them would make a very useful tool . . .

Beck didn't want to smash it up – too much risk of being heard.

'Right!' He walked over to the chair, turned his back and clumsily picked it up with his tied hands. 'You try and get a grip too . . . OK?'

They were standing back to back with the chair held between them.

'Now, hold on and *walk*!'

The chair's maker would have used glue, of course, but that had been a long time ago. Glue can perish . . .

They walked in opposite directions, muscles straining, teeth clenched. Pain sparked in their shoulders from the unnatural force on their arms. And then, suddenly, without warning, the chair came apart. They staggered across the room, each clutching their pieces of wood.

'Now we're talking!'

Beck had part of the seat, and a leg, and one of the struts. The end of the strut was pointed, where it had gone into a hole in another leg. That was what he had wanted. They pulled at it again so that the strut came free, and Beck was left with a pointed, cylindrical piece of wood the length of a school ruler.

'Turn round again . . .'

Once again he studied the knots around Samora's wrists for the likeliest weak point. He turned his own back and, clumsily and from memory, worked the point of the strut in between the two bits of rope that he had chosen. He felt it dig in and gave the wood an extra twist to push it in even further.

'It's working! I can feel it!' Samora reported. The knots were being forced apart by the wood, which exerted more pressure and leverage than Beck's fingers ever could. All at once the wood fell to the floor and Samora stepped away, shaking her hands. The last remains of the knots fell off and her hands were free.

'OK! Let's do you!'

It took her much less time, using the strut with free hands, to get Beck free. He flexed his shoulders to ease his muscles, which were protesting after being tied back for so many hours. He felt the blood flow back into his muscles.

'And *now*,' he said, 'we find a way out.'

Chapter 21

First Beck tied the rope around his waist – 'Just in case!' he muttered dryly.

Then he picked up one of the chair legs, which was sturdier than the strut, and went to work on the floorboards.

There was only one gap wide enough to accommodate the leg, so that was the only place he could work. He dug the leg in as far as it would go and pulled, levering the piece of wood up against the floorboard.

It wasn't easy. He didn't want to pull too hard in case the leg snapped. They had three other chair legs to work with, but someone outside might hear something. And the floorboards had been nailed down for a long time. They were in no hurry to move.

He gritted his teeth and pulled, and pulled again. Sweat began to flow down his forehead and into his eyes. The wood shifted, one reluctant millimetre after another.

Finally it shifted upwards. Samora and Beck could both get their fingers under it, and they pulled with all the strength of their arms and legs. The board came away with a groan of protesting nails – squealing like an angry elephant, Beck thought.

There was no reaction from outside, and they looked triumphantly down into a dark space – a space about twenty centimetres wide.

'You're skinny,' Samora said, 'but you're not that skinny.'

'Same again, then . . .'

With the first board, Beck had been able to jam the leg into a narrow gap and use it as a lever. Now that the gap was wider, that wasn't possible. He thought for a moment, then knelt down and pulled his shirt off over his head.

'Hot work?' Samora asked.

Beck just smiled and lay down on his front next to the gap. He wrapped the shirt around the top of the chair leg and carefully inserted it into the gap between the boards so that the wrapped end was below the board he wanted to prise up.

Then he took hold of the leg firmly in both hands and jabbed it sharply upwards against the bottom of the board. It hit the wood with a muffled thud. The cloth of the shirt absorbed the sound in case anyone was listening outside the hut.

'It shifted,' Samora reported.

Beck grunted and repeated the action. Then again, then a fourth time. The board finally popped up by a centimetre.

It was all that Samora and Beck needed to get their fingers underneath and lift it up. The wood creaked and groaned again. Beck felt sure they must be able to hear it back in Johannesburg. Still no angry shouts from outside, though. They pulled the board away, and now they had a space just wide enough for them to edge into, one at a time.

Beck put his shirt back on and poked the chair leg into the gap, back and forth. The hut was raised off the ground so that things like snakes would go under rather than into it. The problem with that was there might actually be a snake under it now.

But he couldn't feel anything with the end of the stick. Beck reached down and rapped the dry earth with it a couple of times, just to make his point.

'Snakes will generally get out of the way if they know you're coming,' he explained to Samora – then suddenly realized that he'd forgotten for a moment which of the two of them had actually been born in Africa and grown up in a wildlife park.

'Except for mambas.' Her teeth flashed white in the dark. 'They'll go out of their way to *attack* you. And they're deadly.'

Beck had just been about to lower his feet into the gap. He paused, then decided, *What the heck*. He slid down until his feet touched the ground. The floorboards were now at waist level. He lowered himself further and further, holding his breath because the gap was very narrow.

Soon Samora was behind him, and the pair started to crawl towards the edge of the hut, their hearts thumping in their chests . . .

Chapter 22

The space beneath the hut smelled of cool, dry earth and wood. Beck peered ahead, towards the compound. Through the steps he could see the truck that had brought them, parked to one side, and the other buildings. Some had lights on, some were dark. He couldn't see anyone about, though he could hear voices, and somewhere a radio was playing music.

He twisted round to look in the other direction. He could see the edge of the building, a couple of metres from where he was. Beyond it there was enough moonlight to show dry grass and bushes a short distance away, but there was open ground in between. They could run for the cover of the bushes, but if – *if* – anyone happened to look, then they would be spotted.

It was a risk they had to take.

'Come on,' he whispered. 'Mind the mambas.'

They both started to crawl through the shadows, over to where the open ground began. Beck was still waving the chair leg ahead of him. He couldn't see the ground clearly and he didn't want to put his bare hands on anything that might sting, bite or slow down their escape if they broke free. One bite from a snake and they would be in big trouble, out in the bush, with no medical help.

Emerging from under the hut, Samora stopped close behind him, and they looked over towards the bushes. They would be out in the open for about ten seconds.

'Ready?' Beck asked. He jammed the chair leg into his belt. It was sturdy and a handy length – it could be a useful tool; better than having to pick up random sticks along the way. 'OK, let's—'

A gunshot cracked through the darkness and made him jerk his head round. Then another. The second sounded slightly different, which meant that someone was firing back. Then a whole succession of shots tore the night apart. This wasn't just people letting off a few rounds for kicks. This was a gunfight.

Beck and Samora stared at each other, wide-eyed, in the moonlight.

'Think your dad's people have found us?' Beck asked.

She shrugged, as baffled as him. 'Or the police, or the army . . . Poachers have a lot of enemies. Including other poachers.'

The pair knew that it might not be wise to show themselves straight away.

'Let's stay hidden and see how this plays out,' Beck whispered. 'If it's the good guys, great – but if it isn't, then we need to be ready to run.'

They poked their heads round the edge of the hut. The poachers had spilled out of their building and were cautiously circling the compound, eyes straining to see in the gloom. Every now and then one of them spotted something, and raised his gun to fire off a volley into the night. Yellow flame spouted like a dagger from the end of the barrel.

Sometimes there was returning fire, always from a different direction. It looked like the compound was surrounded. Beck glanced behind him again, back the way they had been planning to run. It didn't look like anyone was attacking from that direction.

'Hey, that must be their car,' Samora said suddenly. She tugged at his arm to show where she was looking.

It was way over to one side, and Beck hadn't noticed it before. It was dark metal against a dark background, so it was well hidden. He could only see it now because moonlight shone off the few reflecting bits – a glimpse of bonnet, a flash of bumper. Suddenly, like looking at a magic picture, his brain pieced it all together – and his heart sank.

It was the black Jeep that he had last seen in Johannesburg – which meant that it was James or, more likely, the large man with him, the one who looked like a Silverback, who was now attacking the poachers.

Either way, it meant that Lumos had caught up with him.

Again.

Chapter 23

'What is it?' Samora asked.

Beck realized he had muttered something under his breath. 'Long story, but we haven't been rescued.'

How the *heck* had the Silverback caught up with them?

'We should get over to those bushes and keep going,' he added quickly.

Samora didn't ask why. There was no time for discussion, anyway.

'Come on – follow me,' Beck whispered, and they quickly ran across the open ground, away from the compound and the black Jeep.

Beck scanned the shadows as they ran, keeping an eye open for any accomplices that James might have brought with him.

Then they were amongst the bushes and had to slow down, picking their way through carefully to avoid detection.

The gunshots and shouts faded away behind them. They paused for a moment, ears straining. Suddenly a car door slammed and a powerful engine revved. It came from the direction of the black Jeep – it was closer than Beck had realized. They heard the crash of gears as it reversed and turned round. The driver didn't bother with headlights, which would have provided a handy target for any gun-toting poachers still around. The Jeep roared off into the night, smashing its way through any shrubs and bushes in its way.

Then, finally, there was only the silence of the night. The usual insect song poured into their ears until their brains tuned it out into the background.

'OK,' Samora said. 'I think I'm due an explanation.'

'I think so too,' Beck agreed. 'But first we should get going. We crossed the border, didn't we?'

'Yes. We're about, um, ten miles inside Mozambique . . . Not more than that. But we're still in the Kruger National Park. Any rangers should be able to help us.'

'Yeah, but finding a ranger station would be like looking for a needle in a haystack. Plus we don't have passports and we're in another country,' Beck pointed out. 'Even the friendliest ranger will automatically radio our presence to the authorities.'

Samora's eyebrows went up. 'And that's a bad thing?'

'Yes,' he said firmly.

Beck knew from bitter experience that Lumos had tentacles everywhere. He wouldn't feel safe until he was back with Al and Bongani and Athena.

'Well, there are checkpoints on all the roads,' she said, 'but no fence or barriers so that the animals can move around freely. If we head across country, we should be OK.'

'Cool. We'll do that.' That definitely suited Beck. Staying away from the roads also meant that there was less chance of the Silverback cruising by and picking them up.

'But, Beck, if we're not going straight to the

authorities – how long will it take us to get back to where we want to be?'

He thought out loud: 'It was a three-hour journey, but it was all pretty rough. They didn't use proper roads so they couldn't have travelled fast. Thirty miles an hour?'

'Or forty, maximum. Not more, in a rusty old truck like that.'

'So we came between ninety and a hundred and twenty miles. Now, say we walk at three miles an hour for ten hours a day – with breaks . . .'

Samora swallowed, but she didn't complain. 'Thirty miles a day,' she said.

'So, three days to walk ninety miles. Four to walk a hundred and twenty.'

They both paused to consider the implications of a four-day trek through the Kruger National Park.

'We'd better get moving,' Beck said.

Samora didn't argue. She just asked: 'Which way?'

Chapter 24

Beck looked up at the sky. He hadn't yet had a chance to admire the stars. It was a sight you never got back home in London, where streetlights washed the starlight out of the sky with their bland shade of orange. Here they were a hundred miles from the nearest streetlight and the stars were clearer that he'd ever seen them – millions of them, in all directions, shining down upon the Earth like jewels.

Beck sometimes thought it was the most beautiful sight in the world.

A thick band of light ran across the sky. At first glance it looked a bit like a long cloud, until you examined it more closely and saw that it wasn't just millions but *billions* of stars. It was the Milky Way, the galaxy that Earth's sun was part of, seen side-on.

Back home, or anywhere in the northern hemisphere, Beck would have been looking for the Plough. Find that and you can find the North Star, which doesn't move across the sky but always stays in the north. Once you know where that is, you can navigate in any direction.

But you can't see it from the southern hemisphere. The Earth gets in the way. Instead, Beck ran his eye along the Milky Way until he came to the Coalsack. It was a dark patch, like a hole in the field of stars. It wasn't really a hole – Al had told Beck that it was a vast cloud of interstellar dust, 600 light years away from Earth, blotting out the light of the stars behind it. That was a whole lot cooler than a hole, Beck thought.

Once he had located the Coalsack, he could find the Southern Cross. This was a collection of four stars nearby. They always reminded Beck of a small dagger, with a short handle and a long blade pointing upwards. The stars at the tip of the blade and the right-hand end of the hilt were the two brightest in the sky.

The Southern Cross was tilted over by a couple of

degrees. Beck squinted and held his hand up vertically to measure. He drew a line in his head across the sky that extended the line of the hilt, heading down towards the horizon. When his mental line was about five times longer than the hilt, he stopped. Then he noted the bit of the horizon that was right below it.

That bit was the south.

He turned ninety degrees to his right.

'We go west,' he said. 'We've got a couple of hours of darkness left. We'll get as far away as we can while they can't see us . . .' He trailed off.

'Yes?' Samora prompted.

Beck bit his lip. 'I know how to survive pretty well in—'

'I know you do.'

'I mean, I know how to survive in most terrains pretty well . . . but I've not been here before and there's going to be a ton of things I don't know about this terrain. Like the hunting patterns of some aggressive predators. And those things you only get wrong once.'

Samora chuckled. '*You* keep us alive; *I'll* handle

the indigenous wildlife here. I know their habits. Deal?'

'Deal,' he agreed gratefully. It was, he reflected, an unusual reversal of roles, but he was very grateful for it.

And so they set off into the darkness.

Chapter 25

As they walked, Beck told Samora everything he knew about Lumos.

'But I don't know how they found me . . .' he finished.

They walked a few paces in silence while Samora digested everything he had said.

'Radio tracking.'

'Huh?'

'It's how we keep track of herds, or individual animals, or even birds. Like that elephant, remember? We fasten a small tracker to them. With the right equipment you can find them on the other side of the world. So you can certainly track people the same way.'

Beck's brow creased as he thought. 'So when

would anyone have had time to plant a tracker on me?'

'I don't know. When was the last time you were with someone who isn't me or Al or Athena or my father?'

'Well . . . the lodge, I suppose. Then . . . the helicopter? The pilot? No, we didn't go near each other . . . Anyway, the guy I mentioned found us before that, in the township . . . And the only place we had been before that was the airport.'

And there had been no time for anyone to plant a tracker on him, had there? Beck was ready to push the idea out of his head altogether . . . when he remembered.

He had been pushing the trolley through a crowd, and there had been that particularly hard bump, just once. It had made him feel like a pinball.

'OK . . . Hang on.'

He stopped and looked down at himself. The sun was still below the horizon, but only just. Sunrise was approaching and all the world was grey, including his own body, but he could make out his shape.

He started to pat himself down. Surely he would

have noticed something sticking to him . . . Or someone else would have.

It couldn't be his pockets – he would have noticed
when he put his hands in them. It couldn't be stuck
down his waistband – he would certainly have
noticed someone doing *that*.

But . . .

There was one pocket he didn't use. His top shirt
pocket. He slid his fingers in – and they brushed
against something small and plastic.

It was like a SIM card, nothing more than that. It
didn't have any flashing lights on it and it didn't go
beep. But it was clearly electronic, and Beck had
never seen it before in his life. He held it up.

'This?' he whispered.

'That's the kind of thing.' Samora's voice was
equally hushed, even though she realized that the
device probably wasn't transmitting sound. 'They
have to be small. Like I said, we fasten them to birds.'

Beck dropped it and raised his foot. 'Just in case
you're listening,' he said, 'we found you.'

And he brought his foot down. It crunched very
nicely.

He was surprised to find that he was breathing heavily. It had really got to him: the knowledge that he had been carrying a bit of Lumos around with him all this time made him feel dirty.

'Eew.' Samora was staring at him.

'What?' He started to pat himself down again, convinced she must have seen a second tracker.

'That means you're still wearing the same shirt you were wearing after a twelve-hour flight, and the whole day after that.'

Beck stopped patting. 'Yeah, well . . .' He fought the urge to sniff his armpits. 'I didn't have time to change it this morning.'

'All boys are the same!' Samora joked.

They turned to go.

'And I did change my underwear,' Beck added dryly.

'Good!' she replied as he ground the pieces of the tracking device a bit further into the dirt.

Chapter 26

They walked with their backs to the sunrise so they didn't see it come up. They were just aware of an orange light washing over the landscape around them, making the shadows of night slowly evaporate.

It should have been a beautiful sight . . . but to Beck it was bad news.

It meant that the day was going to get hotter and that they were going to get thirstier.

The poachers hadn't given them anything to drink, so their mouths had been dry even before they set off. The excitement of escaping the gunfight had been enough to keep them going for a while. But as Beck explained about Lumos to Samora, he had been aware that his mouth was getting dryer all the time.

She must have been feeling it too, because her questions had slowly petered out. When she did talk, he heard it in her voice. Her tongue was thick with dehydration, sticking to the roof of her mouth.

Samora was the first to say it out loud.

'I could really do with a glass of water.' She tried to make it sound like a light, throwaway comment.

'Uh-huh.'

They could both have done with something to eat too – they hadn't eaten since lunch the day before – but they could go for much longer before collapsing from lack of food. That wasn't the issue. The issue was water, and it wasn't just a question of being thirsty. Thirst was uncomfortable, but people can live with that. There is more to lack of water than just being thirsty. There is dehydration.

'*Three weeks without food, three days without water!*' That had been something an instructor had once drummed into Beck, over and over again. 'That's as long as a human being can go without two of the three most important things.' (Beck had quickly asked what the third was, and the man had grinned. 'Three minutes without air. So don't go getting stuck underwater, Beck!')

So three days without water. Max. And those three days assumed you weren't exerting yourself or using a lot of energy – certainly not walking across the veld during the heat of a southern African day.

At least they were dressed for it, though. They still wore their sensible safari outfits. But without water, those were the clothes they would die in. As they dehydrated, their organs would pack up, one by one, until eventually their legs would no longer have the strength to propel them forwards.

Then their guts would start to cramp up so that they could barely stand up. Next their minds would begin to go – their brains would shut down; they would become delirious, hallucinating – no longer able to think straight.

And then they would just lie down and die a dazed, agonizing death. Or the grim reaper might come more swiftly: a passing lioness might devour them for dinner. At least that would be quick.

At that last thought, Beck bit his tongue, as if to jolt himself awake. The one thing any survivor had to have was a positive outlook. You have to tell yourself that you *will* get through whatever crisis faces you. Mentally going through the best ways of dying was not showing a positive outlook. If he kept thinking like that, then the battle was already half lost.

And so he looked around at the ground. By now it was light enough to see things clearly. He scuffed at it with the toe of his boot, then bent down and picked up a dusty pebble.

'Breathe through your nose,' he told Samora as he wiped it on his trousers. 'You lose moisture in your breath. You keep more in this way.'

He passed her the cleaned-up pebble. 'And put this under your tongue.'

She took it, then looked at him quizzically. He was already searching around for a pebble of his own. He dusted it off and prepared to pop it into his own mouth.

'Makes you salivate,' he said wryly. 'Keeps your mouth wet.'

Samora's mouth moved as she rolled the pebble around, and then both eyebrows went up and she nodded. It was working.

'Doesn't mean you're getting any more water, though, does it?' she said, removing the pebble for a few seconds. 'You're just reusing what's already in you.'

'True,' Beck admitted, 'but it's a start. Come on. Pebble back in and let's get moving.'

Chapter 27

We need water.

The words kept flashing through Beck's mind. And each time, he sent them on as a kind of prayer.

He knew that, without water, they were in big trouble.

He had learned to pray from his father: each night at bedtime his father used to kneel and ask for God's hand on his son's life. Since then he had often prayed – and not just in sticky situations. And the amazing thing was, so often it had worked. Well, he was still here, wasn't he?

Please? Beck added.

They pressed on westward. At least now they could see where they were going. It also made navigating more straightforward. The principle was easy. The sun had risen in the east and, this being the southern hemisphere, it would move round to the north of them as the day progressed, and then drop down towards the west.

The Earth took twenty-four hours to rotate once – a full 360 degrees. Which meant that, every hour, the sun would have moved fifteen degrees. Of course, the poachers had taken their watches, so neither of them had any way of telling when an hour had passed. They had to estimate, based on the distance they travelled.

Beck assumed they would achieve an average walking speed of about five kilometres per hour. He would pick a landmark on the horizon and estimate its distance. Then they would walk towards it, and pick another, and so on, until they had covered about five kilometres. This meant that the sun would be a further fifteen degrees on from when they had last looked at it. In this manner the pair could estimate which way was west, and keep going.

And all the while, schemes for getting water ran through Beck's mind. If they came to a dry river bed, even a dry stream bed, he knew the best places to dig to find water lurking beneath the surface. There were several kinds of fruit you could eat – if the right kind of trees were available.

He scanned the horizon. This was savannah country – trees grew on these grasslands, but not densely enough to form any sort of forest, or provide shade for them to walk under. The only one he recognized by sight was a buffalo thorn – dark brown, fifteen metres tall. Its tough, thorny branches were used as fences for cattle corrals – but it bore no fruit.

And because he was looking at the horizon, he failed to notice what was at his feet – until he almost trod on it.

'Hey, look!' Samora said.

Beck had only just avoided tripping over a pile of brown balls of dung, each the size of a child's head. The ground around them was scuffed, and the tracks continued in a wide line that crossed their route diagonally. Beck instantly recognized them: elephant tracks. Their broad flat feet didn't sink into the ground – they were designed to spread the elephant's immense weight. So the prints were shallow, flat depressions the size of wobbly dinner plates.

Beck felt his spirits soar. He cocked an eyebrow at the horizon and then up to the sky.

Not quite what I was thinking of, but thanks!

He crouched down beside one of the balls and poked it with a finger.

'Beck!' Samora protested. 'Do you know what that is?'

'Yup. It's the drink we wanted.'

'But . . . it's elephant dung!'

'That's what I said. When I was with the Maasai in Kenya, they showed me this as an emergency way of getting water.' He picked up one of the balls. 'Elephants eat a lot of plants and drink a lot of water – plus they have a very fast digestive system. I mean, look at this.' He prodded the ball of dung: it was a matted bundle of chewed grass and branches, glued together by the juices from the elephant's guts.

'I know,' she said. 'That's why they get colic so badly. But you're still—'

'Which means,' Beck went on, 'the water stays in the . . .' He waved the ball by way of illustration.

'Dung.' Samora filled in the missing word with distaste.

'Dung. And if you get it fresh enough from the elephant's backside, it can be almost sterile. So that means you can squeeze it and drink the fluid.'

And then, because he knew that a demonstration was always much more persuasive than words, he tilted his head back, held the ball above his mouth and squeezed.

'Beck, no!' Samora almost screamed, but it was too late. A steady trickle of yellow water dribbled out of the dung and into Beck's waiting mouth. He grimaced, but kept squeezing until the ball started to crumble and bits fell onto his face.

'Mm.' He smacked his lips and grimaced. It might be sterile, but it had also passed all the way through an elephant and had acquired a certain flavour along the way. 'I . . . uh, I was forgetting: it does help if you hold your nose while you do it.'

Samora looked as if she might faint.

'Seriously . . .' Beck picked up another ball and held it out to her. It was time to stop joking and get rehydrating. 'If we don't get fluids, we'll die. And this is fluids.'

He saw in her eyes that she believed him, but she still hesitated. He knew from experience that there were all kinds of mental barriers to get over before you squeezed fresh elephant poo into your open mouth, so he didn't push her. He simply waited while she ran through all the options and came to the inevitable conclusion.

If she didn't want to die, then she had no choice.

Samora tilted her head back, held up the ball of dung and squeezed. With her free hand she held her nose shut. And she drank the liquid that came out.

Together they studied the dung that was left on the ground. They looked at each other.

'It would be a shame to waste it,' she said.

Beck nodded, smiling. 'That's my girl! And the best place to carry water is inside you,' he told her.

And so they picked up the rest of the dung, wringing out every drop of disgusting, life-giving fluid.

'It could be worse,' she said as she finished her last mouthful. She threw the dung away and wiped her mouth on her sleeve. 'It could be insects.'

'Yeah, they're pretty disgusting too,' Beck said with a laugh. 'But don't worry – we're not eating insects.'

He gazed over the land that lay ahead; he could see no sign of human life.

'Well,' he added, 'not *yet*.'

Chapter 28

A low rumble echoed across the veld. Samora and Beck glanced at each other.

'Lions?' she asked, smiling, though she knew exactly what it was.

'Or my stomach?' Beck replied.

Their stomachs were sending them frequent and clear messages. *The water was lovely, guys, but we need food.*

The elephant dung fluids had helped them to keep going. Beck's senses felt sharper, more alive, and there was an extra spring in their steps as they continued their steady trek back towards the border.

But they couldn't ignore their stomachs for ever, especially now that they were getting so many loud and regular reminders.

It didn't help that Beck had set such a rapid pace. Hurrying was unusual both for him and for Samora.

Yes, previously there had been times, travelling through a hostile landscape, when speed had been important. In Alaska he and Tikaani had had to cross some mountains to fetch urgent medical help for a badly injured Al. But then, hiking across the Sahara with Peter, or across the Kimberley with Brihony, it had been more important just to reach their destination. It took as long as it took. Hurrying just burned energy and used up water.

This time, though, they had company, and they had to stay well ahead of both James and the poachers. So they had kept up the pace. And they were now getting hungrier and hungrier.

They would keep going for another hour, Beck decided. Then he would make a real effort to find food. It might just be grubs living under the bark of a tree, but he would find something.

'Hey, come on,' Samora said suddenly. 'We're not that close to death, are we?'

Beck looked at her in surprise, but she smiled and nodded upwards. He saw vultures circling overhead, but then realized that they were drifting over to a spot on their right. They dropped down into the long grass and disappeared from view.

Immediately Beck changed direction. 'There's something dead over there.'

Samora quickly caught him up. 'It might have been dead for days. It might be crawling with flies.'

'Then we'll leave it.' Eating flesh that was old and rotten would be a death sentence. 'But if it's fresh – well, we'll become scavengers too.'

'Uh-huh. But keep an eye out for hyenas – they're also scavengers, and aggressive ones at that.'

Beck nodded. Hyenas were the size of a large dog, with jaws so powerful they could bite through bone. You did *not* mess with them. If hyenas had already staked a claim to whatever they were heading for, then he and Samora would leave them to it.

But when the pair reached the spot where the vultures had landed, there were no hyenas in sight. Instead, the scavenging birds were all flocking towards the remains of a dead zebra. On its hindquarters they could see deep gouges and bite marks from whatever had killed it. The legs were intact, but the throat had been torn out and the skin over the rib cage had been ripped away so that the bones were exposed.

The vultures thrust their long necks into the body and tore out chunks of flesh. Beck knew that the feathers around their necks were short and stiff so that they didn't get matted with congealed blood and intestinal juices. A long tangle of intestines had been pulled out of the body. It looked like a glistening, bloodstained hose that someone might use to try and inflate the carcass. Inside the gaping wound, the other organs lay like a heap of rubber bags.

Beck ran at the vultures, waving his arms. 'Hey! Hey! Get off!'

The vultures flapped away indignantly, in a kind of hopping dance, using their wings to take clumsy leaps across the ground. Vultures never defended their catch if a bigger creature came along. Instead, they would bide their time and sweep in later to devour any gruesome leftovers.

Beck paused for a moment to admire the beautiful zebra. He was glad he hadn't seen it being chased and torn down by predators, dying in pain and fear. But there was no point in getting senti-mental. This was how it happened in the wild. Animals did not die peacefully in bed, surrounded by friends and relatives.

Plus, he and Samora needed to eat – or they too would end up on the menu.

'We still don't know how long it's been dead,' Samora said matter-of-factly.

Beck knew that a girl raised in the Kruger National Park would have the same practical attitude towards food. 'Nope.' He crouched down to study the dead animal more closely. The animal scent was over-powered by the rich, hot smell of blood and innards. 'It doesn't smell rotten – the vultures wouldn't be eating it if it was bad.' He waved a hand to brush a fly off his face. 'And if it had been killed more than a couple of hours ago, there'd be maggots here . . .' He paused, before adding, 'It'll be safe to eat.'

He noticed that Samora was running her fingers over the bite marks on the zebra's rump. 'What are you thinking?' he asked.

'Judging by these marks, I'd say it was killed by wild dogs. If they're still around . . .'

She let that sink in while everything Beck knew about African wild dogs ran through his mind. They were more like wolves than dogs. They were similar in size, and they hunted in packs. Usually, what they chased, they caught.

'People think of lions as the top predator,' Samora told him, 'but when they hunt, they're successful only thirty per cent of the time.'

'And wild dogs . . . ?'

'Eighty per cent.'

'OK. So let's make this quick.'

Chapter 29

Making it quick was easy to say – not so easy to do.

'We can't just tear the meat off with our fingers,' Samora pointed out. 'Or teeth,' she added.

Beck had a brief vision of them sticking their faces into the mess of the zebra's guts like the vultures, and chewing.

'We have an improvised knife right here.'

'We do?'

'Kind of.'

Beck pulled the chair leg from his belt and considered it. It made a useful club but it had no sharp edge. He could break it in two, and the wood would splinter and that might work. But the edge wouldn't be as sharp as he wanted it, and he would have broken his club.

Then he looked thoughtfully at the zebra's blood-stained ribs. They would be perfect.

'We just have to think a bit smart,' he said. 'Can you grab me a rock? Something heavy that you can just lift. And keep an eye out for any dogs.'

While Samora did that, Beck braced himself with his feet apart. He gripped the chair leg with both hands and jammed it in between two of the zebra's ribs, right at the base where they joined the animal's spine. Then he heaved.

He felt something shift, and then, with a loud crack, one of the ribs broke away. It was still joined to the zebra's breastbone at the other end, but now Beck could hold it in both hands and twist it to work it loose.

After a few attempts the entire rib came away in his hands. It was slender and curved, the length of his arm.

'Will this do?' Samora asked. She had found a lump of stone the size of a small football. Bits of earth still clung to it from where she had levered it out of the ground.

'Perfect. Hang on . . .'

'Oh, thanks!' she replied, struggling under the weight.

Beck jammed one end of the curved rib into the ground, then the other, so that it formed a small arch.

'I'll just take that . . .'

With a bit of fumbling he managed to take the rock from her. He stood over the rib, aimed, and let go.

The rock hit the rib and bounced off. The rib fell over, still intact. They both looked at it for a moment.

'OK, that was a trial run . . .'

'Bones are pretty strong, Beck,' Samora pointed out. 'Otherwise they'd break every time the zebra fell over.'

'So let's apply a bit more force. Hold it steady?'

This time Samora took the rib and held it against the ground, both hands wrapped around one end. Beck wasn't going to rely on gravity again. He lifted the rock and brought it down with all his strength.

The rib shattered into three pieces.

'Yes!'

Beck picked up the middle bit. It was about ten

centimetres long and both ends were sharp and jagged. 'That's better!'

He fingered one of the ends. The bone made a sharp point.

'Pointy,' said Samora.

'Pointy, but not cutty. It needs sharpening.'

At least he now had something to work with. He placed the tip of the piece of rib against the rock that lay on the ground, and dragged the bone back towards him. He did this over and over again, while Samora waited patiently. Slowly a sharp edge started to form. Every minute or so he would stop and check it, rubbing his thumb crossways across it to avoid getting cut.

'Could you see if there's a short length of stick around – like a thick marker pen size?' he asked Samora.

'Finder of sticks and rocks – that's me.'

Eventually Beck was satisfied that the bone was as sharp as it was going to get. If he worked it any more, then it would start to crumble. The problem was, it was now all blade. He couldn't get a grip on it without cutting his fingers.

But Samora had found a short stick, about as thick as two fingers. She handed it to Beck.

'Perfect! Thanks.'

Back in their prison, when they had managed to undo the poachers' knots, Beck had wrapped the ropes that had tied them around his waist. He still had them. Now he unwound one of them and used the bone blade to cut off a length.

Finally he used it to split the end of the stick and then inserted the bone into this incision. Next Beck wrapped the short length of cord around the end of the stick to hold the bone blade in place, so that only half of the cutting edge stuck out.

Job done. Now that he had a knife with a blade and a handle, he could get to work.

Chapter 30

Beck chose a point on the zebra's hindquarters that was well away from the damage caused by its killers. It was also good and meaty, with no bone to complicate matters.

The tip of the bone knife easily pierced the skin; then Beck could work it back and forth. The skin yielded beneath the blade with each stroke. He cut a flap of skin and peeled it back. The meat he now exposed was fresh, red and glistening. He carefully and methodically began to cut away chunks, each one no bigger than a clenched fist.

He passed the first to Samora. She carefully took the lump of flesh and held it up to examine it.

'I ordered mine medium-well,' she joked. 'There's no way I'm tipping.'

'No time to light a fire,' he said apologetically, 'and even if we could, I wouldn't. We're still too close.'

Samora just nodded. He was right. The poachers could easily spot the smoke from a fire.

'Oh well.' Beck held up his own piece of meat. 'Down the hatch.'

He bit into it, hard. He felt the zebra's blood ooze out of the flesh into his mouth. It tasted of iron. The meat was strong and tangy, like eating raw beef but with a much more intense flavour. He had to work his teeth hard to get through the flesh, but it then went down quickly.

They both ate one more piece, then Beck spoke through a mouthful of blood and meat. 'Let's not have any more until we find water. Eating too much protein will dehydrate us even further. We've got some energy inside us now, so let's use that to get moving, and try and find more water on our route. We'll take some of this meat with us for later.'

With that, he continued cutting and slashing at the carcass so that they could fill their pockets for the journey that lay ahead.

But talking of water had given Beck another idea.

This was going to be messy, though.

He rolled up his sleeves, knelt down and pushed his hands into the mess that was the zebra's organs. Feeling about for the stomach was like rummaging about in a pile of slippery rubber balloons. Soon his arms were covered with slimy blood and juices, and the mess of organs sucked and gurgled under his hands.

The stomach was easy to find because the throat led straight into it. When he pulled it out, it writhed between his hands like a rubber sack full of water, quivering and squelching. He held it up triumphantly.

'Pass me the knife, Samora.'

The stomach was connected to the throat at one end and the zebra's intestines at the other. He cut through both ends to free it. The remains of the zebra's last meal splattered then dribbled out of both openings. Beck squeezed the stomach to remove every last bit that he could.

'And what are we doing with that?' Samora had worked with plenty of dead animals, torn apart by other creatures. She was used to this and she wasn't turning green. But she looked curious.

144

'You'll see when we find water . . .'

Suddenly, on the wind, they heard the distinct sound of barking dogs. The zebra's killers were still in the neighbourhood.

Beck and Samora both paused. Then Beck quickly slid the chair leg through the two openings of the stomach and held it across his shoulder. It was the easiest way to carry something slippery and floppy, and it kept a hand free. He tucked the bone knife into his belt.

'We should press on,' he said grimly.

Chapter 31

The river was thirty metres from bank to bank and cut its way across the grassland. On the far side some antelope were bending down to drink. The bank on their side was churned up by countless animal foot-, hoof- and claw-prints, though none of their owners were about.

'That is the most beautiful sight I've ever seen!' Samora exclaimed.

'Yup,' Beck agreed. 'Sometimes elephant poo just isn't the same.'

They had walked for another two hours with the zebra meat in their pockets. The dogs hadn't appeared. Beck hoped that if they felt hungry again, then they would prefer the safely dead zebra to two very much alive humans.

But he knew that they needed water. Every drop of sweat that they produced was one more drop of water that wasn't inside their bodies where it could help them.

They had come to the top of a small rise and had simultaneously spotted the green banks of a river in the far distance. Another hour of walking and they had reached it.

The ground sloped gently down to the water and gently up again on the far side. The banks were lined with reeds and small shrubs and bushes.

Samora ran forward before Beck could stop her, and knelt down so that she could scoop water up into her mouth.

'Hey!' he called as he caught up with her. He thought of all the dangers that might lurk in African waters. 'Crocs? Hippos?'

Samora stood up, wiping water from her mouth. 'Too shallow for hippos to be hiding. You can see it's not deep. And there's no crocs on the bank, and they'd only be hiding underwater if they thought they'd get a meal. They're more likely to be on the other side, eyeing up those antelope.' She pointed over at the far bank. 'If they don't get attacked in the next five minutes, then there aren't any crocs.'

'Makes sense . . .' Beck found it hard to argue with the voice of experience. 'Just making sure we survive now that we've found this river.'

But he still ran his eyes slowly over the running water, searching for anything that might look like a log but turn out to be something reptilian and armour-plated, with a whole host of teeth and claws.

He unshouldered the zebra stomach, and knelt down to drink some water himself. It was cool and refreshing, and strength seemed to flow from it into his tired muscles. It washed a fuzziness out of his mind that he hadn't even realized was there. He felt more awake and even a little taller when he stood up again.

He surveyed the river once more with a thoughtful eye. They had to get across it. He could see how wide it was – but not how deep. Or how fast it was flowing . . .

He snapped a branch off a bush and walked over to a small raised knoll – the highest point along the bank that he could find. Then he hurled the branch out across the water. From his slightly elevated position he could see it spin round as the current caught it. It was carried away down the river at a fast walking pace. If he followed it on foot, he wouldn't quite be running, but he would be walking pretty briskly.

'We can get across that,' Samora said. She sounded slightly less confident now; perhaps she had visions of being swept away.

'We can, but if it gets too deep or we lose our footing, then we could easily get carried away.' Beck made his decision. 'We should try to tripod it.'

'What? We build a tripod?'

'No,' Beck said with a grin. 'We *are* the tripods. Come on. We need two strong, sturdy branches. They have to be the same height as we are, and they must be able to take our weight if we lean on them.'

They searched among the bushes that lined the bank. It took a while, but finally they both had branches that satisfied him. Beck leaned hard on each for a final check, gripping it with both hands and putting his full weight on it. Neither of them snapped.

149

Beck kicked off his boots and his hands reached for his belt buckle. Then he paused. 'Uh . . . We need to, uh . . .'

'. . . take our trousers off?' Samora asked matter of factly.

He nodded. 'Kind of.'

She turned her back, pulled off her own boots and proceeded to remove her trousers. 'Why?' she asked while she was changing.

'They just make extra drag in the water. And you'll be glad of the dry clothes when you get to the other side. And take your socks off too, but put your boots back on. We don't know what's on the river bed.'

Sharp objects might cut their bare feet, but rocks or gravel could just be slippery and painful.

They stuffed their socks into their pockets and wrapped their trousers around their necks. While they did that, Beck explained how they were going to get across. He was still using the chair leg to carry the zebra stomach. He stuffed it down his back, under where he had tied his trousers around his neck, so that they held the chair leg in place. Then he picked up his branch.

'Ready?' he asked.

Samora took one look at him, and burst out laughing.

He supposed he probably did look funny – boots with no socks, bare, skinny legs and boxer shorts.

'Ready,' she agreed, still chuckling.

And together they edged their way into the water.

Chapter 32

'Eww, it's getting into my boots!'

'Well, yeah . . .'

'I know, I know. It just feels so . . . squidgy.'

There was something horrible about the sensation of water trickling into a dry boot. That was why Beck had deliberately stepped out and made his boots flood straight away. The water felt slick and cool against his skin. He felt it rising up his legs as they moved out into the river.

They moved sideways, facing upstream. Beck was slightly behind Samora. This meant that they could always see anything that might be carried downriver towards them, and if Samora fell, Beck would be there to catch her.

As Beck had said, they were human tripods. They

each had two legs and a branch, so they had three points of contact firmly planted on the river bed. Only one point of contact moved at any time. They would carefully slide one foot along to find a secure purchase. Then the next foot, and then the branch, to catch up. And so on.

'And be careful not to cross your feet, but shuffle instead, so that you don't trip up.' Beck spoke calmly, concentrating on the job in hand.

He had remembered that tip from when he was little: his father had given him a demonstration in a shallow stream – purposefully falling head over heels to make the point. Beck smiled at the memory.

But this crossing was getting harder now.

Close to the bank, the river had been sluggish, and they could just splash their way through it. But as they neared the middle of the stream, so the current increased. It began to pull at them. By the time the water was up to their knees, there was a definite bow wave as it flowed past.

To Beck it almost seemed as if the river was toying with them. As if it was quietly watching, waiting for a mistake; given the slightest chance, it would have them over. The bed was soft mud – he could feel no rocks or gravel that would provide a grip. It would be all too easy for their feet to slide and for one of them to topple, taking the other with them.

The river got deeper – deeper than Beck had expected. If it came up much over their waists, then he knew there would be no way they could avoid getting swept away. They would have to throw themselves to the mercy of the current.

The water rose slowly, soaking into his shorts and then the hem of his shirt. Every part of him below his waist was now being pushed back by the water. To compensate for the force he moved his feet back a little, and pushed the branch forward. The points of the tripod were further apart, which would make him more stable.

'How are you doing?' he called. Samora was a little shorter than he was – the water would be higher on her.

'It's . . . yeah.'

He didn't press the point. She needed to concentrate on staying upright, not talking.

The cool torrent soon reached his waist. The bow

wave thrown up by his body made a sinister gurgling sound in his ears. The pressure was like a giant hand placed flat and pushing harder and harder against his whole body, forcing him backwards.

And then at last the water began to go back down again. At first he wasn't sure, but after another minute there was no doubt: it was back to just below his waist. They were past the halfway point and heading up the other side.

Samora let out a whoop as she realized the same thing.

'Don't let up,' Beck called. 'Keep concentrating—'

Suddenly something wrapped itself around his legs and pinned them in place. The foot he had been edging along was unable to move any further. The rest of his body was already shifting, on the assumption that his foot would be there to take his weight. He stumbled over to one side, and the force of the water hit him. He tried to shift his legs, but the thing under the water slithered against them and locked them together.

With a yell he found himself being pushed back. He had to wave his hands to stay upright, which meant taking the pole off the river bed – which meant that he was even less stable.

Just as he was about to topple over completely, he managed to use the pole to regain his balance. The water surged up against his back, but he was more or less upright. Whatever was around his legs was trying to untangle itself. Beck tried to dance away from it before he realized that he was making the situation even worse. He forced himself to keep still and stared down into the water. Something long and thin was wrapped around his ankles.

It was definitely some kind of fish, not a length of weed. His pounding heart, he prayed that it wasn't a water snake; as soon as it got annoyed, it would strike out at him. Now that he was standing still, whatever it was managed to free itself with a couple of deft wriggles. It flicked away from him over the pebbles.

'Mottled eel.' Samora laughed. 'Probably fully grown – they can reach nearly two metres. And they just love to *eat* boys. They trip them up so that they fall over in the river' – her eyes grew wide as she held back the smile – '*and they never come up again!*'

'Oh, yeah . . . ?'

'Yeah . . . Well, no, actually . . .'

'You mean they're really completely harmless?'

'Well, yes. To humans.'

'Shame,' Beck muttered. 'We could have eaten it.'

They continued to work their way towards the far bank, one step at a time.

Chapter 33

Samora dropped down onto the grass.

'That,' she declared, 'was harder than I thought it would be. Even allowing for eels.'

Beck smiled, though he stayed standing. He paced around slowly, letting the sun and wind dry off his soaked lower half. The antelope – a couple of adults and some smaller young – were clustered further down the bank. One of the adults was clearly keeping an eye on him while the others drank, but none of them seemed spooked.

'It would be even harder for those dogs,' he said. 'I think we're in the clear.' He peered curiously at the antelope. 'At least, these guys don't seem worried.'

'The water is so important to them, they'll let predators get quite close before running. Though in your case, if they feel threatened they come straight for you. Those horns are sharp.'

Beck stepped a careful couple of paces away.

'And, Beck, there will be other dogs on this side, and you're still carrying a smelly bit of zebra carcass to attract them.'

'Aha! And didn't I tell you it was for the next time we get water?'

Samora watched as Beck untied the zebra's stomach and went back to the river. He thrust it into the water so that water glugged through the two openings. Then he pulled it out so that the water came splattering out again, mixed with the remains of the stomach's contents. Beck repeated the process until the water ran completely clean.

Finally he used one of the poachers' ropes to tie a tight pair of half-hitch knots around one of the openings, sealing it tight. Then he filled the stomach up again. The knots held and no water came dribbling out of the end.

'So it's a water bottle!' Samora commented.

'Makeshift, but it will do. Handy thing about stomachs is they're as waterproof as any bottle. And

159

these ones can double up as a pillow too! Could you hold this?'

Samora held the stomach upright while Beck sealed off the other end. Then he tied a longer piece of rope to the two ends of the stomach and slung it back over his shoulder.

'What about the poachers?' she asked while he was doing that. 'And your friend from Lumos? They'll be more persistent than a pack of wild dogs.'

'I broke the tracking device, remember? I'm hoping that means we won't see him again. The poachers . . . Hmm.'

Beck squinted back the way they had come. There were no dust clouds, nothing to suggest a pursuing vehicle, but that meant nothing. The men probably knew the country better than they did. They would know where there might be easier fording places. He and Samora had only crossed the river here because they needed to keep moving. They didn't have the time to go up- or downstream looking for shallower crossing places.

But assuming they had won their gunfight, would the poachers come after them anyway?

'They don't know that we memorized their location – or that we know how to survive out here,' Beck said. 'Hopefully they'll just think we're a couple of kids who'll get lost and die in the wilderness.'

Samora held up her fingers to make air commas. '*Hopefully*.'

'Yeah. Well . . .'

Sometimes hope was all you had. Beck had had plenty of opportunity to learn that lesson. But if there were alternatives, then it was better to go with them. *If* the poachers caught them, they would have no qualms about turning a couple of kids into vulture food.

And that meant they had to keep on the move.

He patted the zebra stomach, which now bulged and gurgled a little with the water inside it. 'We'll take sips every hour and fill it up at the next opportunity. Right now' – Beck waved a hand at the river – 'drink all you like, we'll get a few more pieces of zebra down us and then we'll be off.'

He paused as Samora looked at him with a little smile; then he added, 'Hey, Samora, cheer up . . . this adventure is only just getting going!'

Chapter 34

There was something about putting on dry clothes that always made one's spirits lift. Their boots were still damp, but they would dry off as they walked. Every time they stopped for a rest, they would take them off again and give their feet a bit of air. Otherwise there was a danger of getting a fungal infection that would eventually cripple them – though Beck fully intended to be back in civilization long before that happened.

They walked through the afternoon, with occasional breaks for a rest and a sip of water. Every estimated five kilometres, Beck continued to take measurements from the sun. It wasn't easy because they weren't always heading in a straight line. Sometimes geography got in the way – a drop too

sheer to negotiate or a slope too steep to walk up –
so they had to go round the obstacle. Samora also
contributed her own expertise: she made them give
a very wide berth to a family of hyenas they saw in
the distance.

'They have good eyesight, day and night, though
they're not so good on smell. But even they would
smell those zebra pieces if they got close enough –
so let's not give them a reason to investigate us,' she
told Beck.

Skirting round the hyenas to Samora's satis-
faction must have added a kilometre to their journey,
though Beck felt that was a reasonable price to pay
to avoid being eaten alive.

The hyenas weren't the only creatures they saw,
or the only ones to steer clear of. Samora avoided
the places where lions might be around. They
would probably be resting at this time of day – lying
down, almost invisible . . . until two humans came
stumbling in amongst them. At which point they
would realize that they still felt hungry!

Even vegetarian animals could be dangerous.
Buffalo looked slow and placid, but those horns

could split an intruder in two if the animals felt threatened, and they could run a lot faster than a human. The pair also gave elephants a wide berth, not wanting to give the mighty creatures any excuse to sense danger and charge.

Out here, Beck knew, you only got it wrong once. And as his dad used to say: complacency kills. Always stay alert.

And so they made their meandering way across the Kruger National Park. The sun drew alongside, then gradually overtook them, heading for the western horizon. Shades of red and orange began to make their way into the sky. Beck guessed they had about an hour of daylight before the abruptly falling night of southern Africa.

'We should stop soon.'

Samora sagged in relief. 'No more walking? Yay! And we can make a fire! We can actually cook our zebra meat!'

'Well . . .' Beck looked doubtfully back the way they had come. 'I don't know. The smoke could be visible for miles.'

Her face twisted unhappily. 'Oh, please?'

'Well . . . OK, I may be able to do something.'

Half a kilometre away the ground sloped gently up towards a thicket of trees the size of a football field. Beck pointed it out to Samora.

'Any animal dangers? Lions . . .? Leopards . . .?'

She studied it thoughtfully. 'Probably not. They prefer open spaces. Of course, we won't know until we get there.'

Beck bit his lip, and decided. 'Then that's where we're spending the night. And I'll see what I can do about that fire.'

They pressed on into the trees.

It wasn't long before Beck had found exactly what they needed.

Chapter 35

'So what's so special about this place anyway?' Samora asked.

She and Beck stood among the trees at the foot of a short bank of earth. Above them, a tree lay on its side. Its trunk was pitted with holes – slowly eaten away from within by termites.

'There are no obvious animal tracks, for a start,' Beck said. He'd been glad to see this. It meant that it wasn't a trail regularly used by animals on their way to find water, shelter or food. And Beck knew that it was critical to survival in the bush to avoid setting up camp at a spot used as a route by rhinos, cheetahs – or worse.

'And as you can see, we have branches for a shelter.'

Samora squinted at the fallen pile. 'We need a shelter? The nights are warm – the weather's OK.'

'It doesn't have to be anything fancy – just something simple that will protect us . . . and give the animals something to think about if they want to get at you,' Beck added. 'And it's always better to be inside than out. Warmth, protection and morale.'

Samora nodded. It was true: you always felt better sleeping inside something, rather than just being out in the open, however simple the shelter was.

'OK. So we sleep under this lot . . .'

'We can do better than that, I reckon . . .'

If Beck had been properly prepared for their journey across the African bush, he would have had a machete with him – something with which to cut off the branches and make a proper shelter, with a roof and walls and a platform to keep them off the ground.

As it was, he knew that their accommodation for the night would be more than a little rough and ready.

He scrambled up the bank and ducked under the

canopy of branches. Some of them had snapped off when the tree fell over; those that were still attached to the trunk ranged in diameter from the thickness of his wrist to limbs that he couldn't even wrap both hands around. He grabbed a thin one, and pulled.

'We . . . can' – he gave an extra hard tug on the branch – '*pull* . . . this over . . . to make a roof.'

The branch had been angling away from the trunk. With Beck's weight on it, it now stuck out at ninety degrees to the trunk and sloped down towards the ground. He let it go and it immediately swung back to where it had been. He turned and saw that Samora was biting her lip, trying not to laugh.

Beck unwrapped one of the ropes from around his waist and tied a loop around the branch. He gave the loose end to Samora to hold, and resumed his grip on the branch to pull it back over to where he wanted it. 'Now, take up the slack . . .'

Samora braced herself and pulled on the rope. Beck took it from her and tied it to a thinner branch that stuck out from the trunk. Now it was held firmly where he wanted it. It was joined to the trunk at one end, and the other end almost touched the ground.

'Now we can get smaller, loose branches and pile them up on either side. Plug the gaps with anything else that you can find . . . Then we'll have a shelter. Can I leave you to do that? We can tie them all together once you have them in place.'

'Uh, sure.' Samora studied the branches available with a critical eye. 'And you'll be doing what . . . ?'

'Keeping my promise,' he said with a smile. He searched around for what he wanted, and picked it up – a short, sturdy length of wood that wouldn't break easily. 'You wanted a fire – you'll have a fire.'

Chapter 36

Beck left Samora to wrestle with the branches, and went back down below the fallen tree. He studied the sides of the bank for a good place to start what he had in mind. Then he spotted it, about halfway up.

There was a small hole where it looked like some animal had burrowed its way in. He needed to dig a hole too, and there was no point in expending energy doing that when some animal had already done part of the work for him.

First of all Beck stuck the chair leg into the hole, to make sure it wasn't still occupied. He couldn't feel anything at the other end; just solid earth . . . The hole was empty. Good.

He took the bone knife from his belt and studied the tip. It was sharp, but it was also fragile – it would snap if he used it for what he had in mind. He set it aside and picked up the wooden chair leg again. Wishing he had a proper spade, or even that machete he had been dreaming about, Beck gripped the blunt piece of wood in both hands and rammed the sharper end into the earth next to the hole. He twisted and levered it back out so that a clod of earth tumbled out. Then he repeated the action, again and again.

It took time, and the deeper in he got, the more packed and hard the earth was. He kept going – slowly but surely. He had to exert force to get the chair leg into the earth, but he didn't want to work up a sweat and use up his reserves of water.

Little by little the cavity in the bank grew bigger, until it was wide enough for Beck to put his head into. He could now just use the leg to hack away at the earth at the back of the hole. Then, using his hands, he scooped out the loose earth. Once he'd cleared that, he would go back to using the chair leg for the next lot.

Samora had done her work with the shelter, and came down to watch. 'Anything I can do?' she wondered.

There wasn't really room for the two of them to work on the hole side by side.

'Could you gather up some firewood?' Beck asked her. 'Small sticks, and a few large ones' – he made a circle out of his thumb and forefinger – 'about that big.' There wouldn't be room in the hole he was digging for anything larger.

'OK.' Samora went back up to the tree to start gathering wood, and Beck went back to his work.

By the time he was finished, he had opened up a hole about the length of his arm. There was no point in making it any deeper – he wouldn't be able to reach the back otherwise. But there was one last, important thing to do.

The roof of the hole was about twenty centimetres below the top of the bank. Beck hadn't wanted to leave any less than that in case it crumbled and fell in. Any more, and his plan wouldn't work.

He climbed up the bank and stood above the hole with his feet on either side of it, so that his weight wouldn't make it cave in. He picked up the chair leg again and pushed the sharp end straight down into the earth. He twisted it back and forth to drive it in deeper. It took a minute or so, but slowly, bit by bit, he worked it in . . . and suddenly there was no resistance. He had pushed it through the earth into the cavity beneath.

Samora had built up a small pile of wood and leaves. He selected the pieces he wanted carefully. First he used dry leaves to build up a little nest at the back of the cavity, below the vertical hole he had just drilled. Then he laid smaller twigs over them. He slowly built the pile up, the pieces getting larger and larger until he had a bundle about the size of a football.

The theory was that the leaves would catch almost immediately and help to set fire to the twigs. The twigs would then add their heat to the larger pieces and make them burn too.

'Roast zebra coming up?' Samora asked happily.

'Almost . . . almost.'

'Excellent . . .' She cocked her head. 'No offence, but it seems like a lot of trouble just to make a fire.'

'It's a snake-hole fire,' Beck said. He pointed at the vertical hole. 'That's for ventilation. When the fire gets going, it will suck in air through the main entrance, which will reduce the amount of smoke. Only a very thin column will emerge from here. It should hardly be visible at all. And the flames are totally hidden inside. Plus, it will act like an oven. All the heat will be confined to a small space, so that will speed up the cooking process. Your roast zebra's going to be nice and tender, not charred on the outside and raw in the middle like most open fire cooking. That is, once we've lit the fire . . .'

He stepped back and studied the hole thoughtfully.

Samora looked puzzled. 'Problem?'

'Well, we've got to light it with something, haven't we?' Beck thought wistfully of his beloved fire steel, his companion on so many adventures. It could start a fire anywhere . . . except that it was now lying at the bottom of the ocean.

'OK,' he decided, 'we'll use a drill and bow to get it going.'

'A drill and bow?' For some reason Samora sounded amused. 'That's when you spin a stick to create friction?'

'Yup. The string of the bow goes around the drill

and you move it backwards and forwards. Only you need to have a string in the first place . . .' Beck paused for a moment, trying to remember the last time he had done that. Oh, yes – with Peter, in the Sahara. That time, the string had been made from a handy length of parachute cord.

'We've used up all our rope on the shelter,' Samora pointed out, still smiling, as if it was some kind of joke, 'but maybe we can use our shoelaces . . .'

Beck frowned. Samora looked like she was on the verge of collapsing into laughter.

'Well, I'll go and get the wood we need . . .' he went on.

'This is all very impressive,' Samora said. She reached into her pocket and pulled out something really unexpected. It was small, square and plastic. 'Or you could just use my lighter.'

Beck stared at it.

Then he stared at it for a bit longer.

He slowly reached out his hand to take it. He gave it a flick. A small, hot flame appeared at the end.

'Don't tell me you smoke!'

'No, I don't. But the electricity supply is pretty bad out in the offices of the park. You never know when you might need to light a candle. So, roast zebra?'

'Roast zebra!' Beck agreed. 'You know' – he paused – 'you're pretty handy to have around, Samora!'

Chapter 37

Beck woke with a start – an instant transition from fast asleep to full alert.

He and Samora had nodded off quickly, lying head to toe, their stomachs full of hot food, their limbs tired after a hard day's trek.

They had laid out small branches and leaves on the ground inside the shelter to insulate themselves from the chill of the earth. Beck felt them rustle as he half sat up and turned over.

Something big was pushing its way through the trees, and it wasn't making any effort to hide. A crunch, a snap . . . the popping of sticks on the ground. It had to be some kind of animal. Beck lay there and listened, tensed to wake Samora and flee if it started coming much closer.

But after a while he was pretty certain it was moving away. The noises faded into nothing.

Beck breathed a quiet, happy sigh and began to lie down again. He would try and get back to sleep, though his heart was still pounding with adrenalin. And then he paused.

Was something else moving out there?

He strained his ears, and narrowed his eyes to stare out through the leaves of the shelter. The moon was out and it was almost full, so all the trees were bathed in silver light. There was no colour, just shades of silvery grey, or pitch black in the shadows.

It wasn't exactly a *noise*; more like a *sensation*. He wouldn't have noticed it at all if his senses hadn't been so keyed up by the first noise. He couldn't actually hear anything moving, but somehow he had the impression that something was creeping through the trees. Then, every now and then, a twig would snap or a leaf would rustle, and that would con-firm it.

It wasn't anything like the first thing he had heard – it was much smaller than that. The previous intruder had just walked through the trees without caring who heard. This . . . this sounded horribly like someone furtive.

Whatever – whoever – it was, it was moving slowly from Beck's right to his left. It was impossible to guess its distance, but it was inside the trees, so that meant it couldn't be more than ten metres away.

Beck bit his lip. He and Samora were well hidden here, with the roof of the shelter just looking like a pile of branches.

They shouldn't have lit that fire, he thought to himself. Its small signature of drifting wispy smoke must have been enough to give away their position.

Slowly, gently, Beck reached out for Samora and gave her a gentle shake. She woke with no more than a slightly startled 'Huh?'

Beck quickly put his finger to her lips. She looked up at him with wide eyes, and then silently pushed herself up, crouching beside him and staring out. Beck pointed at where he thought the movement was. She nodded.

Then a section of shadow broke away from a tree trunk. It moved off and emerged into a shaft of moonlight. The silver light painted it into the shape of a heavily built man with a mane of hair – a man Beck had seen before, at the shanty town.

The Silverback had found them again.

Maybe one of them made a noise – a gasp, an inhalation of breath – or maybe the guy was just very, very good at what he did. He froze and his head slowly turned to face them. In the moonlight his eyes were shadows, but his features were pale and clear.

Beck was certain they couldn't be seen through the leaves, but a grin of unholy joy spread over the man's face, and Beck was sure he heard him whisper, '*Gotcha*,' before heading purposefully towards them.

Beck and Samora shot to their feet, bursting through the leafy roof of their shelter.

'*Run!*'

Chapter 38

They tore through the trees. Branches came out of the dark, and slapped and whipped against their faces. Beck held up one hand to shield his eyes. The other was firmly grasping Samora's, though it was hard to say which of them was in the lead.

The Silverback was making no attempt to hide now. Beck could hear him crashing through the bushes behind them, making almost as much noise as the thing that had first roused him.

Occasionally there was a shout: '*Oi!*' or '*You!*' or '*Wait . . .*' And then a curse as he stumbled or encountered a thorny bush. The man was much bigger and heavier than they were. He wasn't designed for running through undergrowth.

The noises behind them receded, but only a little.

Beck could tell they were gaining ground on their pursuer, though it couldn't last. The Silverback wasn't going to stop, and the trees wouldn't go on for ever. Sooner or later they would be back out in the grasslands. It would be a whole lot harder out there.

Their only real hope was to find somewhere to hide, and hide so well that the guy gave up looking for them.

They suddenly found themselves in a clearing. Samora was all for running straight across it, but Beck held her back.

'No, wait.'

The clearing was lit up by moonlight – they would stand out like sore thumbs. He guessed they had maybe thirty seconds before the man was upon them.

'Up here.'

They ran over to a tree a few metres away on the edge of the clearing. The lowest branches were about two metres up. Beck wrapped the fingers of both hands together to make a stirrup. Samora put her foot into it and he shunted her up to the lowest branch. She quickly pulled herself up.

The noise of the Silverback was getting closer. Beck made a leap for the branch and just managed to wrap his fingers around it. He swung himself back and forth until his legs were able to wrap around the tree trunk. That gave him enough purchase to pull himself further up, and then he was beside Samora.

They were both starting to climb, aiming for the thick, camouflaging foliage higher up the tree . . . Then they froze where they were as the man burst out into the clearing.

He gave an expression of disgust as he looked around and saw them gone. He raised both hands and let them fall back down by his sides. Then he stood with his hands on his hips and surveyed the scene more thoughtfully. Next he started to pace slowly around the edge of the clearing.

Fortunately he was heading in the wrong direction. Beck began to relax as the man peered carefully under bushes and up trees. But after about ten metres, he stopped. Beck wondered if the Silverback could hear his pounding heart: he turned slowly and began to retrace his steps.

After only a couple of moments he looked up in

their direction – directly at their tree. He put his head to one side, then began to walk forward again, and Beck knew they had been seen.

'Nice try, kid.' The Silverback strode purposefully to the base of their tree. 'Are you and your lady friend coming down, or do I have to come up?'

'Try it,' Beck muttered. He looked around for a branch he could snap off and use as a weapon.

'I've got all night and all day. I've also got food and water. How long are you going to last up there?'

Beck looked at Samora. He knew the man was right. They were in no state to survive up a tree for any length of time.

He was also pretty sure that if Lumos had now finally got their hands on him, then the game was over. And they wouldn't spare Samora either: she knew the whole story, and besides, Lumos had never shown any sign of caring about innocent bystanders.

But as long as they remained up in the tree, they would stay alive. That was good enough for now.

Of course, if the Silverback had a gun, then he could simply pick them off, and that would be that. But he didn't seem to be armed. This struck Beck as curious, not to mention careless, but he wasn't going to complain. It was the one ray of light in their situation.

If he had a gun, then it was probably still in his black Jeep, which had to be around here some-where. So the Silverback would have to go back to get it. Samora and Beck could use that opportunity to scarper – or at least hide more effectively.

'OK, I've had enough of this . . .'

The Silverback leaped for the same branches that Beck had used to pull himself up. He was taller and could reach them just by raising his arms. Beck waited until he was off the ground, then dropped down a little and slammed his foot down hard on the man's fingers.

The man bellowed and let go. He landed on his backside. 'That was *unnecessary*, kid!' He clam-bered to his feet. 'Are you going to behave or—'

Suddenly the trees at the far side of the clearing shook and parted. The Silverback whipped round – just in time to see a massive rhinoceros strolling into the moonlight.

Chapter 39

This was what Beck had heard earlier, he realized. The big man had moved quietly, but the thing that had woken him up had been walking heavily through the trees. Rhinos didn't tiptoe. They didn't care who heard them.

The Silverback gave a startled exclamation. Beck was even more relieved that he didn't have a gun.

'OK, OK . . .' The man was talking very quietly. He didn't take his eyes off the rhino, and the rhino didn't take its eyes off him. 'You're the expert, kid. How do you make these things go away?'

Beck stared out into the moonlight, wide-eyed, but it was Samora who answered.

'You don't,' she said. 'They've got more right to be here than you.'

'Oh, *thank you* . . .'

Across the clearing the rhino stood still. It lowered its horn and stamped its front foot into the ground, then let out a puff of breath that sent a small cloud of dust up into the air.

Beck knew that this was a warning sign. The rhino sure wasn't happy with the intruder being so close.

If the man had any sense, Beck thought, he would quietly step backwards and disappear into the trees. But he also hoped that the man didn't have any sense.

The rhino solved the matter for him. It let out a deep rumble and came trotting forward.

The Silverback gave a yelp and once again leaped for the branch above his head. Beck raised his foot to stamp on his fingers again, then slowly lowered it.

If this rhino was in a rage, then keeping the man out of the tree could be a death sentence. It could trample him, gore him with its horn or crush him with its powerful feet. Beck couldn't do that to anyone. And so, reluctantly, he allowed the man to climb up into the tree.

The Silverback was now on the lowest branch, clinging on with both arms and legs, and Beck and Samora had climbed up a little higher.

The rhino came to a halt and looked up at the man quizzically.

'Push off,' he said uncertainly. 'Shoo!'

The creature stood its ground, then let out another almighty huff of air. The tip of its horn scuffed across the bushes, and it blew out sharply through its nose again. Beck could tell that it was mad.

The hot blast of its breath smelled of lawn clippings and manure. It prodded the trunk with the side of its horn and the whole tree shook. The man clung onto his branch even more tightly.

Another rumble, and the rhino stepped back. It turned to view them sideways on, and the man took the opportunity to climb a little higher and cling on more securely.

But the rhino didn't give him a chance. It decided to step sideways and rub its length along the trunk.

The tree shuddered again. Samora and Beck clung on tightly as their perch whipped back and forth. Loose twigs and leaves fell into Beck's hair.

Beck wondered if the rhino thought they were all some kind of strange fruit that it wanted to knock down. The animal regarded them solemnly, then decided to give the tree a head-butt. The tree lurched like a ship in a storm, and when it sprang back to its upright position, it almost threw Beck off. The Silverback was almost shaken off his branch, managing to hang on with an arm and a leg.

The rhino gave the tree one more bash with the side of its head, and this time Beck heard the trunk crack. He clung on even more tightly, waiting for the tree to topple over. The Silverback was finally knocked off his branch, and plummeted to the ground, landing at the rhino's feet. In one swift move- ment he picked himself up and fled back into the trees.

The rhino gazed after him and gave a rumble, then ambled slowly off into the undergrowth. As far it was concerned, the threat had gone. It disappeared from view, and the two friends could only follow its path by the noises it made.

Off to their right, an engine roared, and they heard a vehicle racing away into the night.

* * *

As their pounding hearts gradually calmed down, they returned to their campsite.

Beck thought for a moment, then bit his lip and kicked out angrily at the nearest piece of wood.

Samora blinked in surprise. 'What?'

'*What?*' Beck exclaimed. 'We were *stupid*, that's what!' Then fairness made him amend this to: 'Sorry. *I* was stupid. We should have done a whole lot more to stay hidden. I shouldn't have lit that fire. I should have camouflaged the shelter better.'

'Beck, you couldn't have known he would track us down . . .'

'And . . .' Beck remembered the way the Silverback had looked at him through the moonlight. Even though he could barely make out the man's shape, his face had been clearly picked out. He must have seen Beck in exactly the same way. 'He saw me through the trees because he spotted my face. The human face is shiny and distinctly shaped. So from now on we're getting camouflaged.'

He climbed down the bank and crouched to remove a lump of charcoal from the snake-hole cavity. It had been a thickish branch when he put it on the fire. Now it was crumbly and grey.

'Hold your face up . . .'

Samora tilted her head back, and Beck drew the charcoal across her forehead and down her nose. He continued the line down one side of her face. Then he stepped back and studied her thoughtfully, before stepping forward again and adding a couple more random patches.

'That'll do it. We instinctively see two eyes, a nose, a mouth, all in the right order. Even in the dark, those features turn into patches of light and dark. An observer naturally pieces together what he is seeing, filling in the gaps and making out a human face.' Beck paused. 'So this works to break up the pattern recognition.'

He put his head on one side to check his handi-work. He was pretty sure that he had added enough varying pattern to confuse the brain of anyone who happened to catch a glimpse of them and didn't already know that they were people.

He handed Samora the charcoal. 'Do me, will you?'

Chapter 40

They set off to walk through the last few hours of the night. Once again Beck saw the red light of dawn flooding over the grasslands before them. It was the second day of their trek.

They had enough zebra meat left to last them another day. Beck had used the fire to cook it all, so that would stop it from going off immediately.

At mid morning they came to a long belt of baobab trees wrapped around a large water hole that was more like a small lake. It was a very welcome place to break the journey. The two humans weren't the only ones seeking shade and water. Some impala were grazing nearby and they studied them nervously before trotting away.

The baobabs were strange trees. It looked like

someone had planted a row and then melted them. Their bark was smooth and shiny, their trunks very thick. But their fruit was good – the size and shape of a child's rugby ball. The contents made your mouth pucker like you were eating something citrusy, but they were nutritious and filled the stomach.

The zebra-stomach water bottle was still a quarter full. They drank the rest of the water to get it inside them. It tasted pretty horrible, having been in contact with the stomach lining for some time, but they gritted their teeth and drank anyway.

Then they found a shallow part of the lake to fill the stomach up again, with more glugs and gurgles.

The shade of the trees was very welcome and Beck was aware that the full heat of the midday sun lay ahead of them. But they had to press on. Someone was after them, and they had to put as much distance between them as they could, and as quickly as possible.

As the afternoon drew on, Beck was delighted to come across a jackalberry tree growing on a termite mound. The tree wasn't tall, only about three metres, with branches at the very top, covered in dark green leaves, making the tree look a bit like a capital T. It didn't offer much shade, but it had fruit – yellow-green and round, the size of large conkers. Beck quickly shinned up the trunk and pulled some clusters off.

The skin of the fruit was tough – you had to use your front teeth to make a hole, then peel it back. Inside, the flesh was chalky, with a faint taste of lemons, but it was edible.

And below the tree was a termite mound, which for Beck was the best news of all.

It looked like it had been thrown up into the air by some underground explosion, and then frozen. It was steep and pointed, a little taller than Beck. Only two or three termites were in evidence, scurrying across the surface. But Beck knew that inside the mound there would be millions of them.

Pound for pound, termites are more nutritious than vegetables and a better source of protein than beef. This mound was like manna from heaven. Unfortunately, as Beck knew well, people tended not to see it that way. He ran various phrases through his mind, searching for the best way to suggest to

Samora that maybe they should eat some bugs.

'Do you like nutmeg?' he asked conversationally.

Something in his tone made Samora glance warily at him. 'I might. Why?'

'Well, then . . .' Beck picked up a stick. 'You'll like things that taste of nutmeg, right?'

Her eyes widened as she caught on, and to his surprise she smiled broadly. 'You mean, like termites?'

She grabbed the stick from him, thrust it into the mound and twirled it around. When she pulled it out again, it was covered with termites. Their natural reflex had made them bite on and stay with it. She plucked one off and popped it into her mouth.

'I'd never really thought about it before, but they are nutmeggy, aren't they?'

'Uh . . . yeah.' Beck was still taken aback by how quickly she had dived in. He plucked a couple off the stick for himself. 'OK – you've done this before, right?'

'Well, it's not like termites are all we eat in South Africa – we do have shops and things too – but, yes, I do this as a trick with tourists in the park and they always grimace at me!'

Beck smiled.

'I do actually quite like the taste, though,' she added.

Between them they finished off the stickful, and then set off again into the last hours of the afternoon.

They were making good progress, Beck thought as the sun cooled and the sky ahead of them turned red. This time tomorrow, they might actually be back at the Green Force lodge.

Ahead of them he saw a ridge of high ground. The trees and bushes at the top were outlined against the setting sun.

'Camp?' he suggested.

Samora gave it an appraising look. 'There's a lot of cover. Could be a leopard up a tree and you'd never know until he fell on you. But we can check it out—' She stopped, head cocked. 'Hear that?'

Beck listened for a moment. 'Nope.'

Samora crept more slowly towards the trees, then stopped again, hand held up. This time Beck thought he could hear it too. A kind of whimpering noise on the wind. 'Sounds like an animal.'

'It sounds like an animal in pain.'

Beck immediately glanced up at the sky. There were no vultures. If an animal was suffering, it wasn't yet interesting to the birds.

They followed the whimper carefully. And eventually they found the source, deep amongst the trees.

Chapter 41

It was lying on its side in a natural clearing of dry earth – an animal the size of a large dog. Its flanks were heaving, and every now and again it trembled, as if in terrible pain.

And in fact it *was* a dog – an African wild dog.

The lean body at the top of its long, skinny legs was a brownish yellow, striped and patterned in a natural camouflage that would have made it hard to spot in tall grass. It had a wide, blunt muzzle and a pair of ears like round radar dishes that immediately pricked up at their approach.

Beck could tell that it knew they were there.

But it neither growled nor raised its head to look at them. Beck suspected that meant it was too ill to worry about them.

'Oh, the poor thing! Look!' Samora whispered, though they could have talked at a normal volume for all the difference it made.

Beck saw that a length of wire was wrapped around the dog's forelegs and shoulders. The loop was attached by another piece of wire to a branch above it. It meant that the forelegs were drawn up tight to its chest. It couldn't have walked if it tried.

'It's a snare,' Beck said sombrely. 'Someone pulled the branch down to the ground, and tied or pegged it in place. Then they attached the loop of wire to that spring. An animal that stood in the snare would knock the branch loose. It would fly back to its former position, and tighten the snare.'

He had occasionally used snares to catch animals. But only as a last resort, when he really needed food. You tailored your snare to the kind of animal you wanted to catch, and you never just left it around for any old creature to wander into.

'Poachers must have set it. The poor thing could have been lying here for days, dying slowly,' Samora muttered.

'Right . . .' Beck moved slowly round to the dog's

head. Its ears turned to follow his movements. A pair of shrewd, dark brown eyes looked up at him.

'Careful,' Samora said. 'They're about as domesticated as wolves.'

'Wolves aren't domesticated,' Beck pointed out.

'Exactly. This one – she's a female – she won't think of you as master. She'll think of you as prey. Don't be taken in just because she's docile at the moment.'

Beck stepped back out of the dog's line of sight. Dogs believe in dominance. If you're bigger, and looking at them, they might take that as a challenge. He didn't want this one to feel threatened.

'Wild dogs are endangered, you know, Beck . . . We should try to free her,' Samora whispered.

'I agree.' Beck had seen the intelligence in those dark eyes. He didn't want to see them glaze over in death.

He still had the bone knife that he had used to cut up the zebra meat. It was tucked into his belt. He took it out and checked that the blade was still firmly attached to the handle. Then he circled round so that he could approach the dog from the rear. Her ears twitched. She still knew he was there, but if she couldn't see him, he reasoned, then she might not panic.

Beck knelt down and worked the blade into the small space between her tightly bound front paws. He felt the blade press into the wire and snag on it. He began to wiggle the blade back and forth gently, in order to ease the wire loose. The bone was brittle – it might break at any moment.

The dog whimpered. Beck resisted the temptation to give her a friendly pat. As Samora had said, these dogs weren't domesticated. This wasn't his neighbour's pet Labrador, the soppiest and friendliest mammal on the face of the planet. She was a dangerous predator in a temporary alliance with one of the humans who liked to think they ran the place.

The wire was now getting looser. Beck took hold of the loop and gently pulled it out of the groove it had cut into the dog's leg. She grunted, and struggled. Beck lifted the snare off completely. The animal was free. Her front legs scrabbled on the ground as she tried to stand up.

Beck moved hastily away.

The dog staggered and fell forward. Her legs weren't yet strong enough to take her weight.

Samora was beaming ear to ear. 'Good job, Beck. Maybe we—'

The smile became fixed, then slowly disappeared. 'Beck . . .'

Beck lifted his eyes from the dog to follow her gaze.

Green eyes shone in the undergrowth, reflecting back the light of the dying sun. Dark shapes moved. Dead ahead, left, right – in fact, all around. Four, five, six of them.

Beck had forgotten the one important fact about African wild dogs. They moved in packs.

And the pack had returned.

Chapter 42

'Hey,' Beck said. 'Uh. Nice doggy?'

One of the dogs growled, then flinched as he turned towards it.

'Uh. Advice?' he asked.

'Move away from the injured one,' Samora said. 'They'll want to protect her if they think you're going to hurt her.'

The dog that Beck had freed was still struggling to stand on her injured legs, though she was getting stronger. Beck took a couple of slow, careful steps backwards.

One of the dogs had the torn-off leg of an antelope in its mouth. It trotted forward and dropped it in front of its injured friend. She tore into it with muffled yelps of gratitude.

'That's amazing,' Samora whispered. 'The pack looks out for its own. They were getting her something to eat.'

The rest of the pack was slowly circling the two friends. Beck knew exactly what was going through their doggy minds. Their friend was hurt. The two humans were here. Therefore the two humans must have hurt their friend. They couldn't understand that Beck had actually freed her.

'Do they attack humans?' he murmured.

'Rarely.'

'Right . . .' A pause. 'That's not quite the same as "never".'

'No.'

Another pause. Another dog took a step forward, then quickly withdrew when Beck moved.

'Will they let us walk quietly away?'

Samora looked about her. They were surrounded. 'Probably not. One of them will eventually summon up the courage to make the first move. So let's make it for them.'

She suddenly waved her arms and ran at the largest and nearest dog – the one that looked like it had humans in mind for its next meal. *'Hah!'*

The dog leaped away from her.

'Hah! Come on, Beck – you too. *Hah!'*

She ran at another dog, her arms windmilling. Beck joined in. The pack scattered in front of them.

'As long as someone is bigger and stronger than they are, they'll respect them. So we have to be bigger and stronger. *Hah!* This way!'

Shouting and waving their arms, they reached the edge of the clearing. The pack were clustered together on the far side, surrounding the injured dog.

'And now, we just move away . . .' Samora said. She took Beck's sleeve and gently tugged him into the trees.

The branches closed behind him, and when he turned round, he could no longer see the dogs.

'And now we move a bit more quickly.'

They hurried out onto the open ground. The sun was very low now; the landscape was red and dusky. There was maybe half an hour of daylight left.

'And keep moving.'

They walked briskly. There was no point in running at the moment. It would only use up energy.

The important thing was just to put distance between them and the dogs, keeping up a steady pace.

'Will they change their mind?' Beck asked.

'They might. They might realize they're still hungry and could do with a meal. Or they might just forget about us and settle down for the night.'

Settling down for the night was one thing he and Samora weren't going to do anytime soon, Beck realized. Not with a pack of African wild dogs anywhere in the vicinity. They would have to find somewhere a good distance away; somewhere secure and defendable. If the dogs had come across them in last night's shelter, they wouldn't have stood a chance.

He began to think ahead. Maybe a tree – something big and strong with a wide top. A baobab, perhaps . . .

A baying cry sounded behind them. Then a chorus of yelps, then another howl.

'I think they might have changed their mind,' Samora said. 'Run!'

Chapter 43

Long grass whipped against their legs as they fled. Beck didn't want to look back. It would only slow them down. His mind was already picturing the dogs – sleek, dark shapes that moved across the ground like torpedoes, aimed straight at them.

'Can we scare them again?' His voice jolted in time with his footsteps. 'Make a loud noise?'

He still had the water bottle slung over his shoulder. It thumped into his waist with every step he took. He thought of maybe throwing it away, saving himself a little weight. But throwing away water . . . ? Bad idea.

'If they've . . . decided to hunt' – Samora's words came out in gasps as she ran – 'they've found . . . their courage.'

'OK . . .' Beck scanned ahead. The ground wasn't smooth. In the distance he could see clumps of trees, piles of rocks. Maybe they could find a spot that could be defended. Somewhere the dogs could only attack from one direction. If there was something – a branch, a rock – that he could wield, he could keep them off, make them change their minds again . . .

Samora was slowing down.

'*What?*' he asked, aghast.

She bent down, her hands on her knees. He couldn't believe she was tired out already.

She wasn't. She only took a couple of breaths before she straightened up and looked him in the eye. 'We've got to split up.'

'*Split up?*'

'They're a pack. They stay together – hunt together. And that means they can only chase one target. There's two of us. Worst case – they come for just one of us. Best case – they get confused and give up altogether. But, Beck, that means we have to do it now. We've got two minutes, max, before they catch up.'

Beck stared at her with his mouth open. His mind instinctively rebelled against the idea. They were friends. They *did* not split up! They stayed together . . .

But Samora knew more than him about pack dogs. There wasn't time to argue.

'OK . . .' They looked at each other, and Beck realized with a pang that this might be goodbye. 'You know how to get where we're going, right?' he asked. Samora nodded. 'So we'll keep going through the night, and look out for each other when it gets light . . .'

On a sudden instinct, they hugged each other. Then, without any further words, Samora went right, Beck went left, and they ran for their lives.

There was a lump on the horizon that Beck really hoped might be rocks. About a hundred metres further on was a group of trees. Dogs don't climb trees. But could he make it across in time? The rocks it was. If he could climb to the top of those, he should be able to fight off any dog with ideas above its station. His feet pounded on the dry ground. Then, after about thirty seconds, he suddenly slowed down to something not much faster than a jog.

'Come on, doggies . . .' he muttered. 'Woof, woof.' Then he whistled. 'Here, boy!'

He could run faster than Samora. He was taller and his legs were longer – which meant that, if he ran as fast as he could, as Samora was doing, she would be the easy target. She would be slower and the dogs would go after her.

He had to become the easy target. Let the dogs think he was the one they could catch without hurrying too much. There was no way they were going to tear his friend apart if he could help it.

A bark snapped through the darkness behind him. The dogs had taken his bait. Immediately Beck exploded into speed.

'Usain Bolt,' he grated between clenched teeth, 'eat your heart out!'

If ever Beck Granger was going to run like an Olympic gold medallist, then it was now – with a pack of wild dogs at his heels.

Then his foot caught on a root and he stumbled

forward, arms windmilling to keep his balance. He ploughed into the ground, rolled over, and was up on his feet and running again, all in one movement.

But the dogs were closing. Fast.

Chapter 44

They were silent now, committed to the chase. They didn't need to bark. The only sound was Beck's boots pounding on the ground and the air rasping in his lungs. But somehow he could *sense* them behind him – getting closer.

The strange thing was, he couldn't hold it against them. They were doing what it was in their nature to do – hunting prey for the pack. This was how the wild worked. It was nothing personal. They weren't plotting to end his life because he was inconvenient and threatened to expose their lies and stop them making money. In other words, they weren't Lumos.

They just wanted to eat him.

And they were faster, stronger and more numerous than him.

To survive, he was going to have to outsmart them.

Dark shapes moved into the corners of his eyes, flowing over the ground on each side of him. The dogs were alongside. So if they could catch him up, why wasn't it all over? Because, said a logical voice at the back of his mind, they also needed to get into a position to pounce and take him down.

And so, for now, they just encircled him, and hemmed him in – and ran with him. They were in no hurry. They knew that he would be the one to tire first. And *when* he slowed down, they would be upon him in a flash – and that would be that. Beck knew he couldn't keep up this pace for much longer.

The rocks he was aiming for lay dead ahead – more like a mound that had collapsed down on itself: a small cliff face, four or five metres high, with a jumble of boulders lying at its base. The sight gave him a little extra strength. He aimed for the nearest part and forced himself to keep his speed up. His body told him that he was about to run into solid rock; it wanted him to slow down before he hurt himself.

That's nothing to what will happen otherwise, he told his body firmly. *Keep going.*

The nearest rock loomed ahead. Beck prepared himself, then ran and jumped, all in one movement, scrambling up on top of it.

Now he could defend himself. He was standing on a narrow ledge with his back to solid rock. The dogs could only come at him from one direction.

The pack surged around the base of the rocks and broke into confused yelps. As far as the dogs were concerned, he hadn't played the game. The prey wasn't supposed to do this. The first dog leaped up onto the rock after him. Its front paws scrabbled for a purchase on the smooth surface.

Beck lurched forward at it. '*Hah!* Go away!'

He aimed a kick at its head. The dog recoiled and fell back. It twisted in mid-air to land on all fours with a thump.

'Oh, yeah! Round one to the human boy! Who's next?'

There were growls and grunts from below him. Beck peered over the edge. Several pairs of glaring green eyes met his. Another dog tentatively put its paws up against the rock.

'*Hah!*'

The dog didn't climb back down. But it didn't jump at him either. Beck wondered if he and the dogs were coming to an understanding. They wouldn't attack so long as he was still moving . . .

So all he had to do was keep awake all night, and then all day, until Samora finally sent someone to fetch him. At this point that didn't seem likely.

'I need another plan,' Beck muttered out loud.

He still had some water. He even had a lump of zebra meat left. If he threw that to the dogs, would they go away? Or would they just regard it as the starter course? He decided not to throw it. He didn't know how long he was going to be here with nothing else to eat—

Claws scraped on rock. Beck froze, then slowly looked round.

'Oh . . . crud.'

The narrow ledge he was standing on stretched away on either side. It must circle the small hill and drop down to ground level. A dog had snuck round the other side and made its way up. It was only a couple of metres away, and all it had to do was pounce.

'*Hah!*'

The dog flinched, but it didn't back away.

Beck tried again. 'I said *hah! Hah!* Go away! Stupid animal!'

This time it didn't even move. This dog wasn't a coward. It had plucked up the nerve to get this far and it wasn't going to back down now. It lowered its head, almost to the ground, and bared its teeth. Its big round ears were aimed squarely at him.

Get it while it's in mid-air, Beck told himself. He kept his eyes fixed on the dog's, and slowly shifted his feet to get himself into the right position. He crouched down. He would only have one chance. The dog would leap, and when it did, it would be unable to change direction. If he could get under it, lever it away, send it over the edge . . .

One chance. One chance only. Boy and wild animal braced for what was to come.

Then, suddenly, a shot rang out – a high explosive *crack* that split the dusk apart. A section of rock between Beck and the dog exploded into small chips. At the same time he heard the high-pitched *twang* of a bullet strike.

The dog spun round and fled back along the ledge.

The pack beneath milled about in confusion. Another shot, another bullet strike – this time on the rocks below Beck. The pack bolted.

Beck sat down and stared out into the dusk, trying to spot his unexpected saviour. And then his heart sank . . . because, striding over the grass towards him, was the familiar shape of the Silverback.

And things were even worse than he'd feared, for now he saw that the Silverback was being followed by James Blake.

Chapter 45

Beck closed his eyes and banged his head against his knees.

Part of him wondered why he was just sitting there when his arch-enemies were casually strolling towards him. The simple answer was that he was exhausted. He didn't have any more running left in him.

The man approached the rocks and looked up. In one hand he casually held a self-loading, high-powered rifle, with its butt resting against his hip. He wore a khaki shirt and slacks that could have been military surplus.

James had his hands on his hips and a wide grin on his face. He was dressed like a city kid out on holiday – T-shirt, long shorts, sandals.

The Silverback was the one who spoke. 'You're welcome. You coming down, kid?'

Every option ran through Beck's head in less than a second. There weren't many. And the truth was, he was out of luck and out of escape routes, while a man with a rifle stood right in front of him.

'No, thanks. I think I'll stay here.'

'Kid . . .' The man tried to sound reasonable. 'If I wanted to shoot you, you'd be dead by now.' To make his point, he slung the rifle over his shoulder so that it hung by its strap. His hands were free and he held them up. 'Or, if we'd wanted the entertainment, I'd have just left you to the doggies.'

James gave him a friendly punch. 'No, we wouldn't,' he scolded.

The Silverback shrugged. 'Whatever.'

With a couple of swift movements he had clambered up to Beck's level. He held out a hand for James, who slowly and clumsily clambered up after him. Beck tensed to flee, but there really was nowhere he could go. Even if he made a break for it while the man was helping James, he would catch up within seconds.

And yet – the fact was finally sinking into Beck's tired brain – the man had been right. He could have shot him already. And he hadn't.

And so that was why Beck just sat there. Beaten.

James made his way up towards him with a pleased look on his face. 'May I . . . ?'

Without waiting for permission he sat down cross-legged in front of Beck. The Silverback leaned back against the rock face behind him. Beck waited for the other boy to speak.

'I don't blame you for not trusting me, Beck.' James flashed him an anxious smile. 'But this is the new James you're looking at. You helped make me. I owe you big time.'

Beck looked at him sceptically.

'Oh, and this is Ian,' James added, with a nod at the Silverback. 'Ian Bostock. You probably ought to be introduced.'

'Hi,' the man said by way of acknowledgement.

Beck still didn't quite trust himself to say anything polite in return, so he grunted.

James's smile grew wider. 'Wow. Where to start . . .'

'Well, you survived Island Alpha,' said Beck.

'Yes . . .' The smile faded. 'I survived.'

Beck knew that James's mother had died on the exploding rig. He had wanted to stay and help her, even though she wanted to kill him. He had wanted to because it was the right thing to do. He knew what it was like to lose a mother. No one should experience that – not even James, and not even a mother like her.

'I'm so sorry about what happened,' he said, and meant it.

James shrugged. 'Yeah, I know you are. Long story short, I ended up in one of the lifepods and washed ashore on an island. Thanks to you, I knew enough to keep myself alive – though it wasn't easy. But I learned. And one of the things that kept me going was thinking of all the different ways I would like to kill you. There were so many, and I had so long to plan them. I was on that island for two months. Two whole months.'

Casually telling a guy – and Beck was sure James meant every word – that he had wanted to kill him was a funny way of making conversation. But, Beck reminded himself, James had had a funny kind of upbringing. And so he just repeated, 'I'm sorry.'

James broke into a smile. 'You know what? It was the best thing that ever happened to me. OK, I barely made it through the first couple of nights, but there were emergency rations in the lifepod for when it got really bad, and you'd shown me how to get water, and find food, and make a fire – that was the longest, hardest bit, I can tell you – and all the time I was raging. I was furious at you. Sometimes it was like you were right there, standing in front of me, and I'd scream and curse at you for abandoning me to die, and I kept myself strong thinking of all the ways I'd get my revenge.'

James had the grace to look embarrassed.

'And then, one day, I fell asleep with warm food inside me, and when I woke up, the fire was still going, and I already had a little food put aside for breakfast, so I knew I wouldn't be hungry, and it was a beautiful day . . . And I understood that you'd saved my life. All the things you'd taught me in your efforts to keep us all alive. All of us.'

James paused.

'It was like a revelation to me that morning on my own. I suddenly realized that I felt a peace and a happiness I'd never felt before. Despite it all.'

He paused again, as if searching for the right words.

'Here I was, on my own . . . with time to think it all through. For myself. I worked hard, I stayed alive – and the truth is, it was the first proper work I'd ever done. And I had no pressure. No one forcing me to be something I didn't really want to be. No one telling me it didn't matter if a person died as long as Lumos thrived. In other words . . .'

He trailed off and didn't finish the sentence. Beck mentally filled in the blanks. *In other words, no poison from his mother*.

'I still miss her,' James said quietly, as if Beck had said it out loud. 'I mean, she *was* my mother. You don't get over that, do you?'

Beck shook his head.

James was quiet for a moment before resuming his story. 'Life is ugly sometimes. But we only get one chance and I wanted to live my life right. Not wrong. So, when a plane eventually saw the big SOS I'd marked out on the beach – that was another of your tips, remember? – I realized that I had a choice to make. Live *her* way or *my* way. Live wrong or live right.'

'So, what were you going to do about Lumos?' Beck asked.

James paused. 'I didn't have a clue. But I knew I wanted to live differently.'

Suddenly his smile became warm again as he looked over at Ian. 'And I knew that Ian could help us.' He paused. 'Go on – tell him about yourself, Ian.'

Chapter 46

Ian grimaced. Beck guessed he was not the kind of guy who liked to use unnecessary words.

'I worked for Abby, James's mother, when James was just a little kid,' he said. 'She and I – we got close. We even thought of getting married. But I didn't like the direction her life was taking, and I wanted to keep James out of it.' He turned to James and there was a momentary softening in his hard-guy features. 'He was a nice kid . . . And so she showed me the door. But James and I – we stayed in touch.'

James waited for a while, but it became clear that this was all Ian planned to say. So he shrugged and continued with the story himself. 'I told Ian everything that had happened, and he agreed to help.'

Beck thought of how he and Ian had first met in the shanty town, Ian roaring up in the black Jeep and trying to drag him away.

'You have a really funny way of helping.'

Both Ian and James narrowed their eyes slightly.

'Funny or not, kid, we saved your life. And your uncle's,' Ian said.

'When? In the shanty town?'

'In London,' James told him. 'Ian was still with Lumos even if he wasn't working for my mother. He heard that Granddad was planning the big one.'

'The big one?'

'The hit,' said Ian, 'that would take you out once and for all. They'd tried the clever stuff – remember, the whole Caribbean thing was about disgracing you as well as getting you out of the way, so everyone would forget you ... Well, Mr Blake decided he'd had enough pussyfooting about. He was sending some guys in with guns. Middle of the night, kick your door down – *bang, bang, bang* – and that would be that.'

'And so I had to get you out of there,' said James. 'I lured you to South Africa.'

'You could have just warned us,' Beck pointed out.

'And make it clear to Granddad that someone had tipped you off? Nah. It had to be obvious that you were leaving of your own accord. The plan was to get you here and kidnap you in front of witnesses, and then make it appear that you'd been killed – and then we could have the little chat we're having now. But, of course, you had to make things difficult by detouring to the shanty town, and then getting kidnapped by poachers . . .'

'We went through plan A, plan B and plan C,' Ian said. For the first time, he almost smiled. 'You were hard to find. Especially after you broke the tracking device. After that, I kind of enjoyed the challenge. Tracking you the old-fashioned way. Like a hunter and its prey.'

'Right . . .' Not so long ago, Beck and his friend Brihony had been tracking a man across the Australian Outback. It was hard work and frustrating – but, yes, it was fun too, when you looked back on it. Though he didn't particularly like being described as *prey*.

'So what's this? Plan D?'

'I suppose it must be,' said James. 'I wasn't really keeping count. Lumos really *does* think you're dead – or they will do when Ian reports back that he saw the wild dogs tear you apart.'

'Blood, screams . . .' Ian grinned. 'Horrible, it was. Mr Blake will love it.'

Suddenly the smile vanished and he peered into the distance. He began to remove a pair of binoculars from a case at his belt.

James kept talking. 'You're out of the way and off their radar. Which means that we can work together and get back at them once and for all. What do you think?'

Wow, was what Beck thought. He sat back and let it all sink in.

But it wasn't sinking in. The simple fact was, he still didn't trust James. He knew from bitter experience that James could tie himself into knots with his lies, and make it all look so easy. Why should things suddenly be any different now? The fact that this was what Beck wanted to hear made it doubly suspicious.

'So why should I trust you?' he demanded.

James's face fell, like Beck had just kicked his puppy.

But Beck needed to be sure. So far, James had told him a good tale. Now he needed proof.

'Uh-oh,' Ian said suddenly. He was looking through his binoculars. 'Company. And not the good sort.'

Beck and James both scrambled to their feet and strained their eyes to see what it was. The horizon was too dark now to make out any detail, but Beck could dimly hear the sound of engines revving as they lurched across the grass.

'Rangers?' James asked.

'Not in beat-up bangers like those. Nope. I think it's Beck's poacher friends.'

Chapter 47

'What?' James exclaimed. 'No way! They can't *still* be after him!'

'They're not after me,' Beck muttered. The small force approaching was not just a couple of poachers looking out for a pair of annoying kids. This was a miniature army, out for revenge. 'They're after the guy who shot up their camp. You'd have been a whole lot easier to follow, in your Jeep.'

'Yeah. Sorry about that.' Ian didn't sound sorry as he put the binos away.

Beck watched as if in a dream as he slowly unslung his gun and began to raise it. '*No!*'

Ian paused and cocked an eyebrow at Beck.

'You want us to work together?' Beck snapped.

'Then you follow my rules, and one of them is: no killing!'

'Not even guys who are trying to kill you?' Ian asked.

'Not even.'

Ian slung the rifle back over his shoulder and sighed. 'Anyway, I can't take them all.' He scanned the group of rocks quickly. 'And we can't hold this position. OK, survival boy, what's your alternative?'

There were very few. Beck peered across the veld and his eyes lighted on the clump of trees he had seen earlier.

'Run,' he said. 'And hide.'

The trees were further away than Beck had thought – maybe two hundred metres. His legs had barely recovered from his life-saving dash earlier. He actually found himself trailing behind James and Ian as they pelted for cover.

'Did they see us?' James gasped.

'Doubt it,' Ian grunted. 'We'd have been in the shadow. Come on, Beck!'

The poachers were approaching from the east,

and the sun was setting in the west. They would have been looking into the bright light of the sunset and would hopefully have just seen the rocks and them as a black, featureless mass.

'But they'll soon find the Jeep,' Ian added, 'and they'll know we're around here somewhere.'

They kept the rocks between them and the poachers, and staggered to a halt once they were under cover of the leaves. They hid behind slender tree trunks and peered back.

The poachers had encircled the rocks with their vehicles; men were swarming about. It would only be a matter of time before one of them thought of checking the trees. And sure enough, Beck saw faces looking their way. He quickly pulled back. There were no shouts, no signs of urgency, so he hadn't been seen. But when he checked again, the men were already making their way over.

'Fall back,' Ian ordered. Beck and James didn't need telling twice, and they withdrew further into the trees.

They soon came to the centre, where the trees had grown up around what used to be a water hole.

It had partially dried up and was now just a muddy bog.

The sounds of pursuit were getting closer. They could hear men's voices now.

'OK,' Ian said. He unslung the rifle again. 'Here's what we do. You two, just run. I'll hold them off. I can duck and dodge and make them think I'm a small army – maybe I can slow them—'

'They'll kill you!' James said, aghast.

Ian shrugged. 'It comes to us all—'

'No one's getting killed!' Beck snapped. 'We hide, that's all.' He crouched down at the edge of the mud.

'What, climb another tree?' Ian asked sardonically. 'Or just dig a hole?'

'Climb another tree,' Beck said. He straightened up with a handful of thick, sticky mud that smelled richly of earth and rotting plants. He dug a finger into it and wiped it across his face, just as he had done that morning with Samora. 'Camouflaged.'

James looked at the mud with distaste, but he slowly reached out for it.

Ian's eyes lit up with approval. 'Nice one.' He

scooped up a handful and turned to James. 'I'll do you.'

Beck concentrated on himself while Ian took care of James, smearing dark lines over the front of the boy's beige T-shirt. 'This'll stand out like a beacon.' He slapped a lump of mud into James's hands. 'Do your legs too.'

While James did that, Ian took care of his own face.

By then, Beck had already found a tree and was halfway up it. James followed, scrambling up with a boost from below from Ian.

'We shouldn't stick together. I'll find another,' Ian said, moving off.

Beck and James looked at each other silently through the gloom. Beck lay along one branch; James crouched at the point where the branch met the trunk. Being alone with the boy who had once wanted to kill him – and, for all Beck knew, still did – was a very strange experience.

James's eyes were wide and trusting, and Beck so badly wanted to believe his story. But he also knew what a good actor James was.

234

He was torn between wanting to keep an eye on James and watching out for the poachers – which meant turning his back on the other boy. Finally he decided that the poachers were more dangerous, and so he turned round and lay on the branch, looking down at the ground.

And saw the men entering the clearing.

Chapter 48

The poachers stopped at the edge of the trees, and slowly spread out. They moved around the edge of the muddy hole, rifles held out in front of them, peering into shadows beneath bushes and branches.

Beck stayed absolutely still. Any kind of movement could be a giveaway. He wished he had thought to mention that to James.

He had never had to put such faith in camouflage before. Would it work? Would it *really* work? James was right next to him, and he didn't look hidden. He looked like a medium-sized teenage boy with mud smeared all over his face.

But what would he look like from a few metres away, blending into the shadows of leaves and branches? That was what mattered.

The men below talked quietly. Even though he didn't speak Portuguese, Beck could easily translate one tense phrase: *'Ele está armado.'* *He is armed.* The man sounded nervous, and with reason. It was one thing to be on the trail of prey. It was another to know that your prey had a gun, was somewhere nearby, and could probably see you, while you couldn't see him.

The poachers below them weren't the only ones around. Beck could hear others moving through the trees. His heart pounded as a man came into view directly beneath him. Beck could have reached down with a stick and knocked his hat off.

James shifted. A minute piece of bark was dislodged; it dropped right next to the man's feet.

He paused and scanned the area around him.

And then he moved away again.

The camouflage had worked.

The poachers searched for close to an hour. The sun had set and the trees were now lit by moonlight. Their task of finding three camouflaged fugitives had gone from difficult to near-impossible. Beck could hear their voices getting louder and angrier. He wondered what interesting Portuguese swear words he would have learned if he could understand them.

And then, abruptly, the men were gone. A few shouted orders, and they were pulling back. They disappeared into the trees, and Beck could hear them tramping away.

James prodded Beck's foot to get his attention, then pointed down at the ground, eyebrows raised to make it a question. *Shall we get down?*

Beck was pleased that he'd had the sense to keep quiet. Maybe the poachers were only pretending, trying to lure them down . . . He shook his head. Better to give it a bit longer.

But then he saw Ian coming towards them, dappled in the moonlight. He looked up at the tree next to them. 'They've gone,' he told the leaves above his head.

'Over here,' James said from their tree, and started to climb down.

There were no shouts, no sounds of gunfire. And so Beck scrambled back along his branch and followed James down to the ground.

'It worked!' James's face seemed to shine like

the moon above. 'It really worked! It was brilliant!'

Ian clapped Beck on the shoulder. 'Good work, kid. Now, where were we—'

A strange, foreign, man-made scent reached Beck's nostrils. His nose wrinkled. 'Hey, can you smell—'

Whoomph.

A sheet of fire flashed up beyond the trees. It raced away in either direction, orange light flickering through the leaves. In only a few seconds, the trees were completely engulfed by flames. The African nightlife of birds and insects set up an angry squall in protest.

'– petrol,' Beck finished.

The poachers must have splashed their fuel cans all around the edge of the trees, and then thrown a match in. If they couldn't find their prey, they were going for the next best thing. They were going to burn them out instead.

Beck, James and Ian were caught in the middle of a ring of fire.

Chapter 49

Even in the firelight, Ian looked pale.

'Not good. What do we do now?'

'Could we wait it out?' James asked. He stood at the edge of the bog. 'It won't burn for ever, and this bit won't burn at all. There's no vegetation.'

He was right – the flames wouldn't reach them in the middle of the patch of mud. But fire wasn't the only thing they had to worry about. Beck could smell the other enemy in the air. It was already rasping at the back of his throat.

'No, but they'll come right up to the edge, and we'll choke on the smoke. We have to get out.'

He had done this once before, on an exercise. In a natural forest, full of dead wood and leaves, even the smallest fire could turn into a wild, out-of-control blaze. There were places around the world where they set controlled fires every couple of years to get rid of the natural tinder. He and Al had visited Georgia, in the US, where Al had been speaking to locals about conserving a plantation of rare wood. On one of their days off, Al had talked the local fire-fighters into taking him and Beck along on a controlled burn exercise. It had been an eye-opening experience and Beck desperately tried to recall what he had learned.

He turned a complete circle, studying the fire on all sides as the warm breeze blew into his face. The heat of the flames meant that air was rising faster than normal – which in turn meant that fresh air was rushing in from all sides. And that just fanned the flames further and made them even hotter . . .

The Americans had taught him to head for a patch that was already burned. It wouldn't burn again. Unfortunately, that was all on the other side of the flames. They still had to get through them.

There. The flames across the clearing looked a little darker, a little lower . . . All they needed was a small break in the trees so that they could reach that spot – not something you would notice without a fire to show it.

'We'll head that way,' Beck said, pointing. He ran his eyes quickly over to the other two. 'Are either of you wearing anything artificial? Anything that isn't one hundred per cent cotton?'

'This . . .' Ian fingered his khaki shirt.

'Then take it off. Artificial fabric can melt – it's like burning plastic sticking to your skin.'

Ian started to strip down to his vest.

'James?'

'Nope, all natural.' Then, to Beck's surprise, James crouched down and scooped up a handful of mud and slimy water in both hands. He dropped the contents on top of his head, smearing them over his face and working them into his hair. 'We need pro-tection, don't we,' he said, a little indistinctly as he was trying to keep his mouth closed. 'The mud will protect our skin . . .'

'Good thinking,' Beck said. James really had been learning about survival . . . and doing his own research – Beck hadn't taught him that trick. 'In fact, smear it all over.' Beck smiled at James through the smoke. 'You know you want to!'

Beck lay down and rolled over several times. The mud was cold and slick, but he could feel it caking him from head to foot. Like James, he rubbed it over his head and face.

'You too, Ian . . .'

And then they were ready – three mud-caked figures, poised to make a break for it.

'Follow me,' Beck said. 'Run quickly, but carefully too. We're not just going to sprint as fast as we can – we can't afford to trip over or get disorientated. We go with purpose, pace and caution.'

He hoicked up the collar of his shirt to cover his mouth and nostrils. 'And do this. It'll protect against the smoke.' It helped that the shirt was soaking wet from his mud bath. The moisture would block out the smoke particles too. 'Ready?'

'Um . . .' James said. 'How do we know our friends aren't just waiting outside to pick us off?'

Beck drew breath to answer, but it was Ian who spoke.

'We don't,' he said bluntly, 'but if we stay here,

we're dead, for sure. Besides, I don't think they'll hang around. If any rangers see the flames, they'll be all over us like fleas on a dog. The poachers won't want that. They're just letting the fire do their work for them.'

'Yeah, well,' Beck said, 'let's be ready in case they *are* waiting. We can use the smoke, dark and confusion to our advantage. Come on.'

They covered their noses and mouths . . . and then just went for it.

Chapter 50

It went against every instinct in Beck's body. They were running *towards* a fire. The air grew hotter. The sting of smoke in his eyes and on his tongue grew stronger. But there was no other way out.

Even though he had aimed for the spot where the flames looked lowest, they were still completely surrounded by them. The trees were huge columns of fire, roaring and crackling as they were consumed. He steered a course well clear of those. But still, small tongues of flame ran along branches and through the undergrowth. Clouds of burning leaves and cinders blew around them.

It was like running through a minefield, where the mines suddenly show themselves just as you're about to tread on them.

Beck tried to head straight for the point he had picked out, but it was impossible. They had to run from side to side, hopping and jumping one way, then another as fire licked all around them.

The air was roasting hot and thick with smoke, almost unbreathable. Sweat poured down Beck's face and washed away the protective layer of mud. His eyes stung as if insects were attacking them, even though he narrowed them to slits behind his hands. The smoke was too thick to see where he was going.

All he had was his basic sense of direction to tell him he was still heading in the right direction.

And then – *wham!*

Beck cried out in pain as he tumbled forward onto the ground. It felt like someone had just thumped him across the shoulders with a baseball bat. A heavy weight on his back pinned him down. He was dimly conscious of James and Ian running past, not stopping.

He tried to call out to them, but all that emerged was a gasp. He didn't dare draw in the breath he needed to shout. He didn't want that smoke inside him.

246

He twisted round as best he could. A fallen branch lay across his thighs. He was lucky it had only struck him a light blow – a couple of centimetres in the wrong direction and it would have knocked him out.

And then, with horror, he saw that the leaves at the end of the branch were on fire, and the fire was spreading.

No!

He braced his arms against the ground and pushed up as hard as he could. Pain sparked in every joint and in the bruised muscles of his back, but he couldn't shift the branch. He risked another look at it. The fire was getting closer, its heat growing more intense.

Beck had known many types of pain – cuts, bruises, broken bones. The closest he had come to burning was foolishly playing with a hot stove when he was little. That had been enough to teach him to handle fire with respect. And now he was trapped, held down by a weight he couldn't move, and if he didn't do something soon, he would burn to death.

He tried one more shove against the ground,

gritting his teeth, ignoring the pain of his screaming muscles.

'*Aargh!*'

Then a pair of feet appeared in front of him. He gazed up at James and saw a very strange look in his eyes.

And suddenly, Beck was no longer in Africa, trapped in a burning forest. He was on a metal platform attached to a drilling rig in the middle of the ocean. James had been there too, struggling to help Beck shift the metal girder that held James's mother pinned. But it had been too heavy for two boys.

That had been Beck's last glimpse of James – until a couple of days ago.

All at once his mind was back in Africa again, and James was staring down at him. Now it was Beck who was pinned, helpless, about to die.

And then the weight on top of him shifted slightly. Beck turned his head. James was now at the far end of the branch; the end that wasn't burning. His arms were wrapped around it and his teeth were gritted with the effort.

'*Move!*' he shouted. Beck dug his elbows into the

ground and tried to crawl forward. The branch was still weighing him down. He could manage a centimetre or two, but that was all.

'*Keep going!*'

'I'm *trying*!'

'I'm going to drop it – I *can't*—'

And then Ian was there too, blundering back through the smoke. He took in the situation at a glance and went to help James. Between them they lifted the branch free, and Beck crawled forward until he was clear of it.

He tried to stand, but his bruised back made him cry out in protest.

'Help him,' Ian told James curtly.

They stood on either side of him, arms around his shoulders, and helped him hobble through the smoke, away from the burning trees.

Chapter 51

When the trio emerged from the flames, they collapsed, coughing, to the ground. Their lungs rasped, their chests heaved as they gasped for air.

No one spoke for a while.

Then, finally, Ian helped the boys to their feet and they stumbled over to the rocks where the dogs had cornered Beck. They made a handy landmark.

'No sign of the poachers,' Ian commented. 'That's one good thing. OK – you two wait here. Get some rest. This may take a while . . .'

And he wandered off into the night to try and find the hidden black Jeep.

For a while Beck and James just sat there in silence, breathing the clean, fresh air, and watching the blazing trees two hundred metres away. Luckily the flames weren't spreading. The ground was damp enough to act as a firebreak. A column of thick, ugly smoke blotted out the stars above, though. Nothing could have survived in there.

James gave Beck a nudge and a big grin. 'Trust me now?'

Beck was too tired to say much, but he managed to give James a smile in return. 'Yeah . . . I trust you. Thanks.'

Silence again.

'So, what now?' Beck asked. 'You didn't just want to get me out of London to save my life – though thanks for that, by the way. You wanted me here for a reason. Something about getting back at Lumos?'

'Here's what we do now. Your uncle Al goes back to England and tells everyone you're dead. Ian goes back to Lumos and is our man on the inside. I go back to being the spoiled brat of an heir.'

Beck smiled slightly. 'And me?'

'You lie low. Enjoy your anonymity for a change!'

'But . . . you still haven't told me what we're going to do. How are we going to fight back at Lumos?'

'Oh, we've well and truly got them,' James said confidently. 'We've got corruption, we've got murder . . . and we've got evidence.'

'Where?'

'Ah.' James's face fell, but only a little. 'That's the thing. We have to go and get it . . .' He paused and turned at the sound of an engine approaching. 'Good, here's Ian.'

The sight of the two headlights lurching towards them was a welcome one. It meant that the poachers hadn't found the Jeep.

Ian pulled up and leaned out of his window. 'I'm listening in to the rangers' radio traffic. There's already rumours of a fire in the park. First light, they'll be all over us. And that's not good.'

'Why?' Beck asked.

Ian shot him a sideways look. 'Maybe it hasn't sunk in, kid, but you're dead. Let's try and keep you that way.'

James and Beck climbed into the back of the Jeep and Ian set off across the veld.

'OK . . .' The idea was growing on Beck. This could be quite cool. 'So I'm dead. But wait – first we have to find Samora and get back to Uncle Al. He'll be going crazy!'

He suddenly felt very guilty that, what with one thing and another, he hadn't even thought about Samora for a couple of hours. 'She still thinks . . . the dogs got me . . .'

He trailed off, confronted by one face that looked unhappy (James's) and one that was hard and unreadable (Ian's, in the mirror).

'What?' he asked.

'You can't tell either of them, Beck,' James said gently. 'They have to believe it too.'

'No way!' Beck replied straight away. 'They can keep secrets. They can—'

'Beck,' Ian said gruffly, 'do you know how good an actor Samora is? 'Cos I don't. Lumos will check this story inside out and back to front. They'll poke it at every point and they'll do their best to tear it apàrt. One weak link and it all goes to pot. Samora and your uncle both have to believe it, and Lumos have to see that if *they* are to believe it. When it's all over – then, of course, we can tell them.'

Beck groaned. He could see Ian's point, but it felt

so cruel. He knew what it was like to lose those close to you. He didn't want to put a friend through that, especially when it wasn't even real.

And *Al* . . . How could he do this to Al?

'You tell me the plan,' he replied quietly. 'Starting with this place we have to go to get the evidence. And then I decide if it's worth keeping this from them.'

'No,' Ian said abruptly.

'Yes,' James said, and for the first time Beck heard a hint of command in his voice. James had been raised to take over Lumos one day. Someone must have taught him how to be a leader, even if he fought against it at every step.

Ian was silent, and then shrugged. 'You're the boss.'

'One day . . .' James leaned towards Beck with a mischievous smile on his face. He wiggled his eyebrows. 'So . . . Have you ever been to the Himalayas?'

Epilogue

'My name is Beck Granger. I've survived in some of the world's toughest environments. But right now, the rhinos of South Africa are fighting a battle for survival of their own.'

Beck's face filled the screen, his eyes narrowed and steely. His expression showed nothing but total resolve. A gentle breeze ruffled his hair.

The camera pulled back. More of Beck came into view. Behind him a rhino grazed placidly on the grass. Beck turned to look at it for a moment, then faced the camera again.

'Some will say that the fight is already lost – that it's already too late to save them. But if there's one thing I've learned during my adventures, it's "Never give

up". No matter how desperate things seem, never, ever give up.'

The picture froze, then faded to a smartly dressed woman standing in almost the same place Beck had. Unlike Beck, she held a microphone bearing the logo of a news channel. Her face was composed and sombre as she looked at the camera.

'That was the last known footage of Beck Granger, who disappeared shortly after it was filmed, and is assumed dead. Beck was here in South Africa to record a video with wildlife expert Athena Sapera, to raise awareness of the perils that face the rhinoceros. And it's quite possible that even though he is no longer with us, he succeeded beyond his wildest dreams.'

Another cut, this time to a courthouse in Johannesburg. Police were escorting three men in handcuffs into the building; they were surrounded by photographers. The woman's voice continued in the background.

'Beck and his friend, Samora Peterson, were able to track down evidence that has led to the arrest of a major rhino-poaching syndicate. Three arrests have been made so far, with more expected to follow. If the men are found guilty, then Samora will be eligible for a reward of one million rand for the information. A spokesman for the family says that she has already pledged to return the money to continue the fight against poaching.'

Now the scene showed Samora approaching the same courthouse, escorted by her father, Bongani, and a couple of other rangers, chosen for their height and bulk so that they could keep the journalists at bay. In spite of them, the woman with a microphone was able to force her way through.

'Samora! Samora! What was the last you saw of Beck Granger?'

One of the rangers looked like he was about to push her aside, but Samora stopped him. She looked into the camera with eyes that were still a little red and puffy. Her voice was steady, but everyone could hear the huge effort she was making to talk without bursting into tears.

'Beck and I were being chased by a pack of wild dogs. I believe he deliberately made himself a target so that they would go after him and leave me alone.'

Her voice began to shake. 'He was the bravest boy . . .' She tailed off, then continued, 'Make that, he was the bravest *man* I've ever met—'

A ranger moved her away before she could break down completely. The camera didn't follow her.

The scene returned to the woman, now back in the Kruger National Park.

'This station tried to contact Beck's uncle and guardian, Professor Sir Alan Granger. He was too upset to appear on camera, but instead released a statement.'

She read from a sheet of paper.

'*I hope against hope that Beck is still alive, but with each passing day I know that good news becomes less and less likely. I honour Beck's life, the values he lived by, and his total commitment to preserving the world in which we live. I know that his life was not in vain and that he will prove an untold source of inspiration to many others that follow*.'

A final, solemn look at the camera.

'This is Serena Vorster, returning you to the studio—'

The picture vanished as a hand jabbed at the remote control.

In an oak-lined office, a tall, thin, elderly man smiled. He was bald apart from a circle of white hair around the edge of his scalp. His neck was long and gangly and his shoulders were stooped.

Edwin Blake always reminded Ian of the vultures he had seen in South Africa, hovering over corpses. When the old man smiled, his mouth moved a little at a time, as if the separate parts were remembering what to do.

'Show me the trophy,' Blake said.

Ian pulled a khaki safari shirt out of a plastic bag that lay at his feet. It was tattered and torn, and it was soaked in blood. The blood was dark brown now, dried and caked.

'The DNA matches,' he said.

The blood actually *was* Beck's. He had parted with it, painlessly, in a doctor's surgery in Johannesburg. That had been Beck's idea.

The old man took the shirt reverently, as if handling a holy relic. 'Did you see him die?'

Ian shook his head. 'I got there too late, Mr Blake.

But I heard the screams. He was torn limb from limb.'

Blake was silent for a moment. His eyes were closed and he swayed from side to side. He looked as if he was taking a moment to appreciate some beautiful, distant music.

'So Beck Granger is out of our hair for good.' He opened his eyes and passed the shirt back to Ian. 'Burn that, and get some rest. Be back here tomorrow. We have a very great deal to get on with, now that kid is finally gone.'

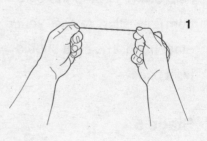

MAKING YOUR OWN LAID CORDAGE

Laid cordage is the term for any rope made from fibres that are twisted together.

Stage 1

Take a long, single fibre. Twist it repeatedly in one direction until it naturally wants to form a kink.

Stage 2

Fold the fibre about a third of the way along. Don't be tempted to fold it in half, as this will give you a weaker finished product.

Stage 3

Grasp the fold between the finger and thumb of one hand. Place the doubled-over fibre on your lap and use the palm of your free  hand to roll it one full roll away from you. You are not trying to make the fibres overlap at this stage; just aiming to twist each strand individually.

Stage 4

Keeping your palm firmly held down, to stop the cord from untwisting, release your other hand. The cord should twist neatly.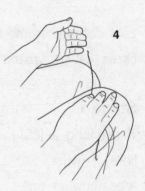

Stage 5

Pinch the cord where the twisting ends and repeat the process until you are 4–5cm from the shortest end. To continue, lay another strand of fibre up to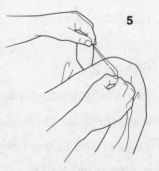

the shortest end and carry on the process as before –
the new fibre will automatically entwine itself into the
existing cord. When you've finished rolling the cord,
just tie it at the loose end to stop it unravelling. If the
cord is too thick to do this, you can tie a separate
piece of cord round the end instead.

Your finished cord will be substantially stronger than
your original fibres, but you can make it stronger still
by folding over the existing cord and repeating the
process. If you do this, make sure you roll the cord in
the opposite direction to the way you started.

MISSION SURVIVAL

GOLD OF THE GODS

Would you survive?

Beck Granger is lost in the jungle with no food,
no compass, and no hope of rescue.

But Beck is no ordinary teenager – he's
the world's youngest survival expert.
If anyone can make it out alive, he can.

MISSION SURVIVAL
WAY OF THE WOLF

Would you survive?

A fatal plane crash. A frozen wilderness.
The world's youngest survival expert
is in trouble again . . .

MISSION SURVIVAL
SANDS OF THE SCORPIAN

Would you survive?

Beck Granger is about to face his toughest survival
challenge yet – the Sahara Desert. Blistering sun
and no water for hundreds of miles . . .

Can he survive the heat and make it out alive?

MISSION SURVIVAL
TRACKS OF THE TIGER

Would you survive?

A volcano eruption leaves Beck stranded
and alone in the jungle. Beck must use
all his skills to survive the dangers of
the jungle – can he get to safety?

MISSION✛SURVIVAL
CLAWS OF THE CROCODILE

Would you survive?

Beck is in the Outback looking for the truth about
the death of his parents. But somebody is willing
to kill to keep the truth secret.

Has Beck finally met his match?

MISSION SURVIVAL
STRIKE OF THE SHARK

Would you survive?

Beck is ship-wrecked and will need all his
survival skills to save his fellow passengers.
The sinking was no accident;
someone wants him dead . . .

Can he figure out who before the sharks strike?

MUD, SWEAT AND TEARS

**This is the thrilling story of everyone's favourite
real-life action man – Bear Grylls.**

**Find out what it's like to take on mountaineering,
martial arts, parachuting, life in the SAS – and all
that nature can throw at you!**

TRUE GRIT

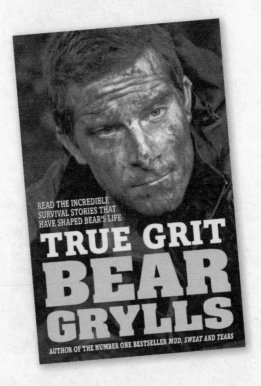

Could you survive in a desert without water?

Would you cope if your ship sank in a storm?

What if your plane crashed in the mountains?

Have you got True Grit?

**Read the true stories of incredible survival against the
odds that have inspired Bear Grylls throughout his life.**

BEAR GRYLLS is one of the world's most famous adventurers. After spending three years in the SAS he set off to explore the globe in search of even bigger challenges. He has climbed Mount Everest, crossed the Sahara Desert and circumnavigated Britain on a jet-ski. His TV shows have been seen by more than 1.2 billion viewers in more than 150 countries. In 2009, Bear became Chief Scout to the Scouting Association. He lives in London and Wales with his wife Shara and their three sons: Jesse, Marmaduke and Huckleberry.